EDEN'S FALL
FALL

Joseph James Pasculli

VICTORY BOOKS

VICTORY BOOKS
333 S. State Street #301
Lake Oswego, Oregon 97034

This is a work of fiction. The characters, incidents, and dialogues are from the author's imagination and not to be confused with reality. Any resemblance to actual events or persons, living or dead, is entirely coincidental.

EDEN'S FALL

Victory Books/ published
by arrangement with the author

PRINTING HISTORY
Victory Books/March 1999

Library of Congress Catalog Number 98-061846

ISBN 0-9669139-0-6

PRINTED IN THE UNITED STATES OF AMERICA

53 70 74 77 80 99 33

TO MY MOTHER
FOR BELIEVING

CHAPTER ONE

A blazing yellow sun hung high in a clear blue sky as the sweltering heat pounded down, without mercy, baking the hard earth below. With no protective clouds to provide even the smallest moments of temporary shade, the concentrated warmth was strongly felt by the inhabitants of Baghdad, Iraq.

On the ground, where there was no escape, the scorching heat was actually visible in a hazy torridity coming off the rocky terrain of the Iraqi landscape. The open, barren flatland spread out as far as the eye could see and beyond, with only a far-reaching highway that cut across the land and the occasional hovel to indicate any signs of life, past or present.

Off in the distance, down the long, straight road, two indistinguishable vehicles appeared over the horizon with the fiery sun behind them. A dusky, blurry cloud of road dust, exhaust fumes, and hot wind billowed out from behind the two vehicles, which accented their approach. As they moved up the road, the vehicles gained clarity and became distinct.

Two white Land Rovers with black capital letters "UN" printed on the hood, roof, rear, and both side doors moved up the road at a medium speed in single file. They contained representatives of the United Nations inspection team sent to inspect suspected nuclear & biological weapons plants throughout Iraq. Their mission was an especially sensitive one as they headed toward one of Saddam Hussein's many Presidential Palaces.

The two Land Rovers were almost identical in appearance and amount of occupants, each vehicle carrying three United Nations inspectors and one indigenous driver. The only difference between them was that the lead one had its windows all rolled down, in an apparent attempt to allow in the outside breeze created by the moving vehicle.

The three U.N. inspectors in the lead Land Rover were all feeling the effects of the Iraqi climate, and were of different nationalities. One American. One English. One French. All men. They wore inexpensive business suits, minus the suit jackets, which lay on the seats beside them. Even with their neckties loosened and shirts buttoned down, the three inspectors sweated profusely. Despite the conditions, they were all still enthused about the job at hand.

The American inspector was seated up front next to the Iraqi driver – who being a native of the land was unaffected by the lack of creature comforts.

"We're trading Land Rovers on the way back. This heat is unbearable," the American inspector said after kicking his foot against the broken air conditioner.

"Perk up, old boy," the English inspector said from the back seat in a typical stiff upper lip manner. "We'll be there shortly and then you'll forget all about the temperature."

"I still can't believe Saddam finally gave in. It doesn't make any sense after all this time," the American inspector said in a leery, anxious tone.

"It was only a matter of time, old boy. Once he understood the United Nations wasn't going to be bullied, what choice did he have?" the English inspector said more genuinely enthused.

"He may be a madman, but he also knows there is no way he would profit from a war with the rest of the world," the French inspector added.

The Iraqi driver wasn't as optimistic about the trip as the inspectors. He knew the American had good reason to be suspicious of Saddam's change of heart.

"We are almost there, but I would not get your hopes up too much. I fear that this is as far as we will get," the Iraqi driver informed them.

The two Land Rovers slowed down as they closed in on the Presidential Palace as it appeared over a rise in the road. The occupants gazed through the windshield in awe at the massive structure set out in the middle of the desert. A long red concrete wall surrounded the entire circumference of the Palace, one of Saddam Hussein's many extravagant indulgences brought about at the expense of the Iraqi people.

Due to the lack of a natural breeze, the Iraqi flag was wired up to remain viewed in full scale. It was raised upon both peaks of two tall towers that were constructed on the sides of the main structure. The tower tops were shaped in the same green mushroom style as the Palace roof.

The highway, a direct route leading to the Palace, ended at the Palace front gate. Five heavily armed guards were posted there, and their reaction to the U.N. Land Rovers was not one of welcome expectation, but rather that of hostile intruders. They pointed their automatic weapons at the Land Rovers and forced them to an abrupt halt.

Everyone in the Land Rovers, including the drivers, put up their hands. They were all shocked, except for the Iraqi driver, by the sudden turn of events.

"Could it be that they weren't told we were coming today," the American inspector offered as a possible explanation.

"That is impossible. They would have had to been notified. No one shits in this country without Saddam's approval," the French inspector retorted crudely.

The Iraqi driver turned his head toward his passengers, cautious not to make any sudden moves.

"I shall go talk to them and inform them that we are expected," the Iraqi driver said as he carefully opened the door, keeping his hands raised above his head, then stepping out of the Land Rover.

The inspectors themselves remained in the Land Rover, while the driver talked to the Palace guards. They watched through the windshield as the guards appeared to be communicating with the driver without any overt hostility, but without lowering their weapons.

One of the guards headed over to the guard post station.

"I don't like it. They had no idea we were coming," the American Inspector said.

"That guard appears to be going to communicate with someone at the Palace," the French inspector speculated.

"I'm sure this will all be sorted out. Just a misunderstanding, I'm sure," the English inspector said optimistically.

The American inspector shook his head in a doubtful gesture as he thought to himself that the driver was right. This would be as far as they would get and that the entire trip was an entire waste of time.

After a few moments at the guard station, the guard walked back over to the others, and the information he passed didn't change their demeanor any. They pointed their weapons at the driver, and one guard motioned with his gun for him to get moving.

The Iraqi driver signaled to the driver of the other Land Rover to turn around before he got back into his own Land Rover.

The three inspectors assaulted the driver with a barrage of questions before he could even sit down.

"What is going on? What happened?" the American inspector asked first.

"Where are we going now? Didn't they know we were expected?" the English inspector asked next.

The driver didn't answer them right away. He was more concerned with smiling at the guards without making any sudden moves. He sat down, started the engine, and made a U-turn right in the middle of the road, which brought the other Land Rover into view in front of them.

"Please, please.   I beg for your patience. But I think we should get out of here as quickly as we can. I will tell you this. They were not expecting us," the Iraqi driver explained nervously.

The inspectors remained anxiously patient, feeling somewhat satisfied, as they pondered their position to themselves.

The two Land Rovers moved away from the Presidential Palace at a hurried pace.   The Land Rover with its windows rolled down pulled in front of the other one and retook the lead position. Both vehicles traveled at a much faster speed then before as they quickly put a good distance between them and the Palace.

The blazing sun, which was now in front of them, blinded their vision as they drove back the way they came. The driver, in the first Land Rover, shielded the sun from his eyes by using his hand raised above his brow as he squinted his way down the road.

About a half mile up the road where the Land Rovers headed, two Iraqi army jeeps were blocking the way, parked nose to nose. Outside the army jeeps, stood ten men wearing Iraqi army uniforms and armed with automatic weapons.

The two Land Rovers were forced to another sudden halt at the blockade. The ten men in Iraqi army uniforms quickly surrounded the Land Rovers, pointing their weapons at the occupants – who must have thought they just experienced a sort of déjà vu.

Everyone in the Land Rovers, once again, raised their hands above their heads. They were understandably surprised by this latest halt. The three inspectors in the lead Land Rover remained calm, but were getting impatient.

"What the hell is going on here?" the American inspector asked angrily.

Even the English inspector was quite miffed.

"Yes, there is certainly going to be a lot said about this. I can tell you that."

"I cannot believe the arrogance," the French inspector added in haughty voice.

For the first time, the Iraqi driver appeared to be truly afraid. The fear in his eyes was accented by the beads of sweat that rolled down his forehead.

"This is very bad."

The reflection of one of the soldiers, who moved in close to the driver's side, shone out in the Iraqi driver's eye and revealed the source of his fear. The soldier, Andrei Yusov—a ruthless Russian mercenary dressed in an Iraqi army uniform, but clearly not an Iraqi—smiled at the driver showing his big white teeth. He had stark white hair, which was mostly covered by an army cap, while his eyes were covered with goggles.

Yusov signaled to his men, who immediately forced everyone out of the two Land Rovers. Seven of Yusov's men where natives of Iraq, and they lined up the six inspectors and two drivers on the side of the road.

The inspectors all mumbled among themselves, while the two drivers prayed fearfully. The three inspectors who had the comfort of the air conditioned Land Rover all began to perspire both from fear and the heat.

"What do you think this is all about," the American inspector from the air-conditioned Land Rover asked the other American inspector in a hushed voice.

"It's a bunch of bullshit," the American inspector answered in an irritated voice that caught Yusov's attention.

"Be quiet and stand still!" Yusov commanded.

Everyone shut up, except the American inspector from the first Land Rover. He made the mistake of getting indignant by stepping forward to confront Yusov. More than likely urged on by the oppressive heat.

"Now see here. We are members of the United Nation and, umf......"

The American inspector was cut off in mid-sentence as an AK 47 gun butt was slammed into his stomach, causing him to fall to the ground in extreme pain. His assailant was Demetri Vadmir, Yusov's right hand man, who was also clearly not an Iraqi, but another Russian and a long time comrade to Yusov.

Yusov had made quite a name for himself (though few alive knew him on sight) since the end of the cold war. He freelanced his expertise to the highest bidder and always delivered. Like many of his expatriates, he felt betrayed by the former Soviet Union. He still believed in Communism and was willing to do anything to show the world that the capitalist dogs of America were the true cancer in the world, poisoning the minds of weaker countries with their foolish dreams of freedom.

"Demetri! Go get the video camera!" Yusov ordered.

Demetri, as always, did as he was told, while one of Yusov's other men put the inspector back in line.

"Gentlemen, if you'll just bear with me for one moment, this will be over very shortly," Yusov said with a pleasing smile.

Demetri returned with the video camera a few moments later and loaded a tape in it so that the inspectors could see the action.

The inspectors all sighed a breath of relief at the sight of the video camera. The American inspector was being held up on his feet with the help of the English inspector.

"Perk up, old boy. Looks like they are just going to hold us hostage," the English inspector said softly.

Yusov just smiled at the inspectors as if to confirm their suspicions.

"I am ready, Andrei," Demetri said.

"Good. Make sure you get the vehicles in the picture," Yusov said.

Demetri stood to the side of the road and aimed the video camera at everyone lined up along the road.

All the inspectors, the two drivers, the seven armed men in Iraqi army uniforms, and the two jeeps appeared in the video camera viewfinder along with a little red dot.

Demetri nodded to Yusov to let him know that he was recording.

"Welcome to history, gentlemen," Yusov said cynically as he gave the signal to his men to open fire.

Before the inspectors could say anything, Yusov's men gunned them down while the camera recorded the carnage.

Their bodies were all held up for a few moments, as the bullets ripped into their flesh, before falling to the ground in pools of blood.

CHAPTER TWO

Two days later, at Fort Lewis, Washington, the video tape of the U.N. inspectors and their drivers being executed was being broadcasted on a television set in one of the many day rooms. On the bottom of the screen, the CNN logo was displayed as the news commentator explained the images in a voice over narration, with only a small identifying picture with his name—John Abrams.

"This shocking video was sent out yesterday to the United Nations and news media around the world," Abrams explained. "The video tape was sent out anonymously and the Iraqi government denies all responsibility. They claim the assassins are imposters."

The television set was mounted on the wall of the large, spacious day room. There were game tables; pool, ping-pong, fussball; beverage machines; soda, coffee, juice; tables, chairs and sofas spread out around the room with the furniture in the middle.

Due to the early morning hour, 4:00 a.m., the day room was nearly empty. Captain Jack Halprin, a Special Forces team leader, sat stretched out on a sofa and listened to the newscast while half asleep.

"This unexpected and horrific turn of events comes on the heels of ever increasing breakdowns in the United Nations Special Commission's negotiations with Saddam Hussein. Saddam still refuses to allow the inspectors into restricted Presidential Sites to check out suspected nuclear & biological weapons plants," Abrams continued.

Halprin's face showed signs of someone who had been suffering from a lack of sleep.

His eyes were wide open, but glassy. There were heavy bags under his eyes and he had a three day beard growth. His attention appeared to be focused on the television, but his mind was somewhere else as the newscast droned on.

The television picture had cut back to the news room with John Abrams seated behind a news desk.

"This latest action has prompted Vice President Kimball to send out a third aircraft carrier, the USS Independence, to join an already formidable U.S. Navy armada in the Persian Gulf. Vice President Kimball—who has been the acting Commander in Chief since the tragic horseback riding accident that put President Robbins into a coma six weeks ago—had this to say at a press briefing yesterday."

The picture cut to the White House press room, with the words: RECORDED EARLIER printed on the lower part of the screen. Vice President Kimball was standing at a podium with the White House Insignia behind him. He was a man of presence, confidence, and intelligence, all tempered with a morality that could be seen by just looking at his face. A true leader.

"First, I would like to start off by saying that our hopes and prayers go to President Robbins and his family in hopes that he will make a speedy recovery. There is however no change in his condition to report at this time," Kimball paused for a moment to clear his throat to indicate that he was moving to another subject.

"Now as for the situation in Iraq. Saddam Hussein denies responsibility for this vile, unprovoked ambush of the U.N. Special Inspectors. Therefore, we are left with no other choice than to ready our military forces for a full-scale strike on Iraq. A diplomatic solution has not been ruled out as talks continue. We must not give up hope for a peaceful resolution to this unexpected tragedy."

As the Vice President's speech trailed off, Halprin's eyes blinked a few times before he dozed off. The Vice President's final words echoed in the back of his mind as the dream began, once more. The dream he tried to forget, but over the years came back to haunt him.

****

The dream always started the same. Vietnam. Ban Me Thuot. The Nineteen Sixty-Eight Tet Offensive. Thirty years ago. Jack Halprin was a snot-nosed seventeen year old kid. Lt. John Halprin, his older brother, was twenty-nine years old and the leader of a twelve man Special Forces A-Team unit that Jack was assigned to. John always looked out for his younger brother and helped him get into the Army after their parents died in a traffic accident a year ago.

The A-Team unit, comprised almost entirely of Rhade tribesmen, made its way up a hill and into a small, knee-high grassy field with a tree line along its border. The top of the hill stretched the length of a football field before it dropped down to a valley.

Lt. John Halprin raised his hand and signaled his men to stop as they reached the small plateau. They all knelt down to take five as they faced outward, forming a security perimeter more out of habit rather than out of concern for their position.

Jack was next to his brother, who was checking out a map as he tried to get a fix on their location. Jack had his sniper rifle in his hands, but was also at ease.

"Hey, bro. What the hell are we doing out here? This is Tet, right? The Vietnamese New Year. So every gook, both North and South, is out banging the gong and chowing down on hot rice and rat meat. There's no reason to expect any action during a cease fire."

Halprin's brother had a more serious attitude about their position.

"Look, kid. For a seventeen year old punk, who lied his way to be in this shit, you are one cocky son-of-a-bitch," John scolded his brother. "I don't care if you are the best sharpshooter I've ever seen.   Fucking-a! Always expect the unexpected."

Jack looked at his older brother and knew by the tone of his voice that he was deadly serious.   Suddenly the team's attention was alerted by the sound of something unseen moving toward them, about four hundred yards down the hill in front of the unit. Something spread out and large.   Everyone in the unit quickly threw down canteen cups and C-ration cans as Lt. John Halprin signaled a silent alert.   They were fairly covered by the thick grass and rocks, which concealed their position as the sound of brush breaking and clanging metal began to surround them.   And fortunately, they had a good concealed view of the area below them.

Lt. Halprin was getting a sick feeling in the pit of his stomach. A unit making that much noise was a helluva lot bigger than he wanted to face--let alone see. It was also to big to run from and to late. He could sense the other veterans on his team feeling the same. It might be time for each to make his peace with god & budha, he thought, as he now regretted letting his kid brother accompany him on patrol. The source of the sound interrupted his thoughts as it revealed what seemed like the entire North Vietnamese army approached towards the team's position from all sides.

Jack used his rifle scope to sight in the enemy. He sucked in his breath and his eyes widened as he spotted out several thousand Vietnamese soldiers now only three hundred yards from his position.

Then something caught Jack's eye. While traversing the scope over the waves of enemy soldiers, he focused in on a tall figure with white hair, directing the Vietnamese up the hill. The white-haired man was looking through a pair of binoculars and spotted Jack and the unit while pointing out his position to his subordinates. Jack didn't realize that it was the reflection from his scope that had given his position away. This left Jack with no choice but to open fire, but not before the white-haired man could get out of the way and signal for his men to attack.

The first shots rang out and several North Vietnamese soldiers fell to the ground as hot lead ripped into them. Pandemonium reigned as barrages of bullets started coming and going from every direction.

Lt. Halprin made his way over to Communication Sgt. Johnson, who was trying to contact the Forward Air Controller just as a couple of bullets blew the M-16 out of Halprin's hands and sent Johnson into the next world.

Lt. Halprin reached the dead Sgt. Johnson as the response came through.

"This is Falcon Two. Come in Alpha Three. Over." The Forward Air Controller's voice rose out of the radio.

Lt. Halprin grabbed the receiver from his dead comrade and yelled into it as he checked his map. "Falcon Two. This is Alpha Three! We got a regiment of gooks moving in fast—only three clicks from Base Camp. We are about to be overrun. I need an air strike on our checkpoint. ASAP. We're popping Blue smoke. Burn everything around our position, checkpoint Sunset Strip. Over!" Halprin threw down several blue smoke grenades about ten yards in front of his position.

"Roger Wilco. This is flight team leader, we have six effectives in your area. Identifying blue smoke. Will stay on your position as long as we can. Over."

Jack Halprin was taking out any North Vietnamese soldier who looked like a leader with extreme accuracy as he sighted through his riflescope. He also searched for the mysterious white-haired man. If he could take out the main honcho, it might buy them some more time.

Lt. Halprin saw what his brother was up to and tried to get him to take hug the ground.

"Come on, Jack. Get your ass down. Suck dirt!" Lt. Halprin yelled to his brother while still propped up on his elbows.

Jack momentarily paused and put his head down as he reloaded. A single shot was clearly distinguishable to him as it zinged past his ear. He instinctively turned his head at the sound of the bullet and saw several others hit John full in the chest. He tried to start back towards his brother, but was slowed down as a bullet ripped into his shoulder blade from behind.

Jack paused briefly with the intense pain, but quickly recovered enough to begin shooting enemy soldiers again. The adrenalin of hate coupled with despair kept him scoping in North Vietnamese regulars and blowing them away. Then, as he looked out for what seemed the hundredth time, he again sighted in the white-haired man. Sweat stung his eyes, as Jack squinted into the scope. The image of his enemy was becoming just a blur to him as he was rapidly losing consciousness due to the loss of blood. He started to pull the trigger thinking "your dead now fucker" to take out the white-haired guy, but before he could fire a blinding white light engulfed everything. Falcon Two's jets were napalming and strafing everything but the small patch of ground around the quickly disappearing blue smoke.

****

Back in the Day Room, Halprin snapped awake as if he was hit by a bomb blast for a second time. The news was still going on about the military buildup in Iraq, and Halprin became interested in what was being said as he tried to focus his still sleepy eyes.

"Along with the present military buildup in the Persian Gulf, a specially trained assault unit composed of marines, infantry, and aviation groups set out for the Gulf early this morning, an anonymous source was quoted as saying," news commentator John Abrams reported.

Halprin sighed, disappointed over not being selected for that team. The sound of the familiar voice of Sergeant Major Sam Parker, Halprin's life long friend, startled him away from the television.

"I know you wanted to go on that mission, Jack. Hell, we all wanted to go, but higher wasn't going to let it happen."

Parker sat off to the side of Halprin on another sofa. He was in his mid-fifties and had an unlit cigar in his mouth, which accentuated his burly features and hard jaw line.

Halprin looked over at Parker with a sardonic smirk as he nodded his head.

"Always looking out for me, huh old friend," Halprin mused.

"Yeah, seems like a pretty good idea, considering you haven't been giving it much thought lately," Parker replied. "When was the last time you slept for more than a couple of hours at a time?"

"It's not that bad," Halprin said as his smirk faded away to support a more amiable expression. "Really. I just feel that I'm leaving something unfinished in my life. Something important."

"What could you possibly have left to prove to yourself-or anyone?" Parker quipped with a sly sigh. "You're a highly decorated soldier with more medals than John Wayne. Several successful missions in the Gulf War, alone. Hell, you can't get every mission that comes along."

"Aren't you just as concerned with

what's happening as I am?" Halprin referred to the newscast. "There's something wrong about the way that Iraqi ambush went down. It doesn't make sense."

"Hey, Jack. Of course I'm concerned," Parker pointed out. "But, I'm not obsessed by it either. I think there's something out of sync about the whole thing, but these things never make any sense and you'll drive yourself mad thinking about it."

Parker paused for a moment to catch his breath and change the subject. "Look, Jack. You need to get away and relax, take it easy. I got the whole team pumped up and ready to go. You're long overdue for leave and I think that it would be a good time."

"I don't know," Jack said as he looked back up at the television, then back at his friend. "I just can't stop thinking that I have to be ready for the unexpected."

"Come on, Jack," Parker pleaded. "It's not like if you stop moving you'll die or anything. Besides, I got the perfect place.

An island paradise in the Indian Ocean. The Seychelles islands."

Halprin nodded, knowingly. The location of the islands intrigued him.

"Weren't you and my brother stationed there in the early Sixties? There is a S.M.A.R.T. satellite tracking station there."

"Yeah. That's right," Parker agreed. "But that's not what I mean. It is a tropical paradise. Supposedly "the" location of the original Garden of Eden. So what do you say? Ready for some fun in the sun with an entire island filled with beautiful native women?"

"All right, I'll go," Halprin said as he laughed good heartily. "Maybe if you get yourself some tail, then you'll get off my back."

Halprin got up and started out the room.

Parker stood up as Halprin reached the exit. "Hey Jack. It's not your job to save the world, just free the oppressed."

"Yes, it is," Halprin said as he stopped and turned to face his friend.   "I'm Special Forces."

CHAPTER THREE

An U.S. communications satellite floated among the stars in the cosmos with the planet Earth below it, off in the distance. Land masses became more distinct and the United States of America became more prominent in a literal map of the world. As the Earth rotated, the continent of Africa and the Indian Ocean passed by, along with a small cluster of rocks—the Seychelles Islands.

There were over ninety islands that made up the Republic of the Seychelles. Uninhabited until two hundred years ago, then only by ex-slaves, Asian traders, and European adventurers—the islands served as a kind of safe-haven for refugees, pirates, and expatriates. Originally claimed in 1756 by the French, by whom the islands were named, the Seychelles stimulated interests in China, India, Russia, Tanzania, Kenya, the Middle East, and America. Located in the midst of a destabilized ocean area of considerable strategic importance, the islands were opened up to major influences from world powers with the building of a U.S. Satellite Monitoring Alert Response Tracking ("S.M.A.R.T.") Station and an international airport on the main island, Mahe', between the late 60's and early 70's.

A massive boom of international tourism gave the islands a more commercial appeal. The Mahe' beaches were always crowded with swimmers, sunbathers, and beautiful island girls with a marina that accommodated everything from sailboats to luxury yachts. The crime rate on Mahe' was almost non-existent, even though drug lords and arms dealers were often present--or more likely because of these factors. In any case, nobody wanted to draw attention to themselves and no one in authority wanted to know anymore than they needed.

The S.M.A.R.T. Station, located on the highest mountains on Mahe', had a large white satellite dish that dwarfed the station by comparison.   An American Embassy shared the same site when it was given an annex sometime in the late 70's after a coup d'etat that almost brought down the then unstable government.

****

Captain Kate Allen, a perky Air Force officer and second in command of the tracking station, walked through the S.M.A.R.T. room with a cup of coffee in her hand. Her shoulder length brown hair was pulled behind her neck and was mostly covered by her officer's cap.

As Kate passed by the long line of manned radar stations and communication consoles—the heart of the S.M.A.R.T. complex—her attention was caught by the exclamation of Communication Specialist Williams.

"What the hell!" Williams voiced echoed out.

"Excuse me," Kate said as she stopped in front of Williams, who was a young man from middle America and startled by her presence.

"Pardon me, Captain," Williams said apologetically. "But I just intercepted a strange coded transmission originating somewhere out of Iran."

"What is so strange about that, Williams?" Kate asked none too impressed. "We're always picking up garbled transmissions, especially with all that's going on in that region right now."

"It's not where it came from, Captain," Williams offered by way of explanation. "It is where it went to that's got me confused."

"How do you know where it went to?" Kate asked.

"I normally wouldn't," Williams confessed. "But I picked up another transmission using the same algorithm, about forty miles north of Mahe'. Somewhere out near one of the uninhabited islands. They must have been responding."

"Isn't there a U.S. exploration boat reported out near there?" Kate asked a little more interested.

"Yes, Captain," Williams confirmed. "But I've been in contact with them and their last position was about twenty miles away from there."

"Can you decipher the transmission?" Kate asked with piqued interest.

"I'm not sure," Williams admitted with some doubt. "It may take some time, Captain."

"Keep on it and let me know what you come up with," Kate said before heading for her office.

****

Kate sat behind her desk, tapping her pen on her coffee cup, lost in thought. It was just before noon but the approaching lunchtime hour was the farthest thing from her mind.

The front door to her office was open and her commanding officer, Colonel Thomas Vanderweel, walked by, then backed up, and stopped in the doorway. He was an affable old man, who believed in doing things by the book. He knocked on Kate's open door and struck his head in the room.

"Going to lunch, Captain Allen?" Colonel Vanderweel asked.

"Huh!" Kate didn't register his presence, right off. "Oh, Colonel Vanderweel. Yes, sir, I am," she said as she put down her pen and stood up.

"Something on your mind, Captain?" Vanderweel asked as he stepped inside her office.

"It's probably nothing, sir," Kate said reluctant to voice her opinion. "I feel silly even mentioning it."

"Well, if it is enough to cloud your mind, maybe you should tell me what it is and we'll see if we can satisfy that curiosity of yours," Vanderweel said with an easy attitude that made Kate smile.

"I've been thinking about the situation in Iraq and the strategic importance of the Seychelles islands," Kate began. "Then there's this coded transmission that Communication Specialist Williams intercepted from somewhere in Iran, apparently directed at one of the uninhabited islands."

"I wouldn't give it too much thought, Captain," Vanderweel said unconcerned. "Probably just a ghost bounce off a cloud layer. You've only been here ten months, after awhile you'll get use to it. As for Iraq, whether or not we make an air strike is not our concern. But if we do I hope we blow Saddam right out of his royal palace. There is nothing to worry about here. This is still a third world country and they know better than to mess with the United States of America," Vanderweel finished and paused to reflect before continuing. "I was here during the Gulf War and the only action we saw was when the aircraft carriers docked in the port."

"I guess you're right, sir," Kate said as she walked around to the front of her desk.

"I know I am," Vanderweel agreed. "You'll feel better when the U.S.S. Nimitz docks for shore leave in several days. They've been out in the Gulf for six months and have just been relieved by the Independence."

"Do you think we'll be going to war with Iraq, sir?" Kate asked with a concerned voice.

Vanderweel got serious as he contemplated his response. "Saddam denies responsibility for the U.N. ambush, but his refusal to allow them in to do their job in the first place is reason enough. But I'm sure Vice President Kimball will make the right choice."

Kate followed Vanderweel to her office doorway.

"I hope it doesn't come to that, but we can't let madmen like Saddam have control of weapons of mass destruction. Maybe there is still a chance he'll see he has no choice." Kate said hopefully.

"You never can tell."

CHAPTER FOUR

The Mahe' beach was alive with action. Sunbathers, tourists, swimmers, islanders were all having fun in the sun. A volleyball net was set up by the shore line, with a game in progress. Ten of the men from Halprin's unit were divided into two teams and played with the usual strenuous, competitive spirit.

A small group of scantily clad island girls, some topless, watched the buffed bodies of the military men wearing only shorts. They were like a giddy bunch of school girls, but clearly young women, impressed by the impassioned players.

Halprin and Parker sat on the beach chairs off to the side with large drinks ornamented with tiny umbrellas. Both seemed very relaxed and comfortable. Halprin laughed at the antics of his men, especially Walker Hunt.

Walker, was a muscular, agile young man, who seemed intent on making an impression on one of the island girls who was watching. Every time it was his turn to return the ball, he hit it back from a variety of increasingly difficult positions. Backwards. One-handed. And finally he jumped forward and did a handstand as he kicked the ball over the net with his feet and scored the winning point.

The island girls all cheered and jumped for joy. Walker made his way over to Mara—the island girl he was trying to impress—while still in his handstand. He flipped to his feet as he reached her and came up facing her. The other island girls all ran over and joined both the winners and losers making everyone forget who actually won the match. The men of Halprin's unit were a tight knit bunch and the island girls pulled them toward the ocean, wanting to cool off in the water. A few of the men egged Halprin on to join them as they headed for the waves.

"Hey, Cap," Reid, the second weapons specialist, called out. "Come on along."

"Yeah, Cap. The water is perfect, here," Fuller, a demolition specialist, added.

"Halprin put his drink down in the sand, adjusted his shades, and leaned back in his chair. "You guys go on ahead. I think I'm going to take a nap," Halprin said.

Parker smiled at Halprin as he got up, which instigated Fergusen, a medic, to needle the old man. "Hey, the SMAJ is actually moving." He said jokingly.

"Ha, Ha, fellows. I'm gonna go get some lunch," Parker said as he held up his hand and shook his head. Then to Halprin. "I'll see you up there later. Get some rest."

"That won't be a problem," Halprin said looking quite relaxed.

Walker and Mara walked past Halprin and Parker hand in hand. Walker smiled at them as they passed.

"Reminds me when I was young," Parker said enviously. "Ain't it grand."

CHAPTER FIVE

Kate was sitting at an outside table on the veranda of the main island restaurant—Chez T'ed—having lunch with Major Joan Harris. Major Harris was the Office in Charge of the marines who guarded both the tracking station and the American Embassy. They had just finished ordering their lunch as the waiter walked away.

Both Joan and Kate were in their early thirties and attractive women. Joan was a blonde, but her female marine cut was mostly covered by her white officer's cap. She was a hardcore military woman. A real G.I. Jane.

"I thought since it's such a beautiful day it would be nice to get out," Kate said not wanting to get to the real reason she had asked Joan there.

"There is no arguing that," Joan agreed as she gazed up at the sky. "But why do I get the feeling that is not why we're down here, today."

"Am I that easy to read, Joan?" Kate asked with a sigh and a slight smile.

"Pretty much. So what is up?" Joan asked.

"This will be probably be the second time today I'm going to feel like a silly twit," Kate said shyly.

"Don't," Joan said. "You should never ignore your instincts. They may save your life one day."

Kate looked a little at ease as she nodded her head and smiled. "Earlier today we intercepted a coded transmission-- coming from Iran, and it seemed to be directed at one of the uninhabited islands. I mentioned it to Colonel Vanderweel, who didn't think much of it, and neither did I until I checked back with Williams, the commo specialist who brought it to my attention."

The waiter returned with their lunch and Kate waited for him to leave before continuing.   Both of them were having Caesar salads.

"Before I left I asked Williams to try and contact the U.S. Treasure Seeker, an exploration boat that has been reported in the area, but he couldn't.   And he wasn't having any problems earlier," Kate said as she finished stating her concerns.

"Any idea what the message was?" Joan asked as she picked at her salad.

"Williams was still working on it when I left and the only thing he came up with so far was that he thinks it's a destination," Kate answered as she started to also pick at her salad.

"Well, I can see why Vanderweel didn't

think much of it, but that doesn't mean there isn't something to it," Joan said offering her opinion.

"Yeah, the Colonel is a strictly by the book type of man," Kate agreed. "But there's also been a lot of recent activity on the island with that mercenary camp Governor Hubert allowed here."

"That son-of-a-bitch would sell his own mother except I'm not sure he has one," Joan said put-off by the mention of the Governor.

"You're probably right about that," Kate agreed as they both laughed a little.

"That slimeball Hubert already sells passports to every drug lord, arms dealer, and low life criminal who can afford his price for sanctuary," Joan ranted getting more serious.

"That reminds me," Kate said as Joan's words triggered her memory. "I have reports that reputed arms dealer Fernando Santiago docked his yacht around the same time that mercenary camp sprung up two days ago."

"Think there's a connection?" Joan asked after pondering for a couple of seconds.

"No," Kate said as she shook her head. "The mercenaries arrived in a private jet."

"I can see your preoccupation with this," Joan said understandingly. "I don't think there is anything to it. Even though I wouldn't put anything past Hubert."

"I feel better, but I still feel uncomfortable with it," Kate said a little more at ease. "At least the Nimitz will be here in a few days."

"That should keep Hubert in line. I don't think he'd try anything too shady with the Seventh Fleet at his back. He doesn't have the balls," Joan said with a laugh that Kate joined in on.

CHAPTER SIX

The mercenary camp was located on the east side of the island. A six foot razor wire fence enclosed the five acre facility, which had a beach front and a single entrance gate. It was originally set up in the early 60's as a prison for rebel dissidents captured while trying to overthrow the then unstable government. But by the mid-70's, the government had formed into a one-party system, the Seychelles People's Progressive Front ("SPPF"), with an elected governor as the head of state who had almost unlimited authority over the islands. Now as the millennium approached, the strategic importance and its safe-haven reputation for illegal activities became the prevailing lure to the islands, even though tourism still boomed.

The low key attitude, where everybody minded their own business and no one wanted any attention drawn to themselves, was just the way the now elected-for-life governor, Marcel Hubert, wanted it. The peaceful existence that coincided with the American military and government personnel at the tracking station and embassy, along with the criminal element that frequented the islands pleased Hubert just fine. He wouldn't have it any other way. But as he rode to the mercenary camp to meet with Yusov, he wondered if hadn't made a mistake. Something about Yusov frightened Hubert and he wasn't a man who was easily scared. He knew Yusov wasn't just training men or involved in a simple arms deal. This was something bigger. Something that once done the world would know about it. Not that that mattered much to Hubert. Yusov and his sponsors in Iran paid extremely well and gave him sufficient assurances that his mission wouldn't interfere with the islands relations with the rest of the world.

But still he wondered.

Governor Hubert's black BMW passed through the mercenary training camp entrance and stopped just inside. The driver stepped out and walked around and opened the back door. Hubert stepped out and put on a white fedora hat, which covered his balding gray hair. He was a short man in his late forties dressed in a white suit. He walked with a black cane but had no limp or handicap.

Hubert walked over to where Yusov was overseeing the training exercises.

Fifty mercenaries of different nationalities were engaged in a variety of training maneuvers spread out over the well-equipped campgrounds. Fifteen of the mercenaries were at the target range on the far side of the camp, near the water. In front of that was an obstacle course, which was being used by another fifteen mercenaries. The rest were engaged in hand to hand combat exercises and general physical training.

"Ah, Governor Hubert. How good of you to pay us a visit," Yusov said as Hubert reached him. "What do you think of my men?"

"They certainly are a fine looking group," Hubert said as he stood next to Yusov while looking at the men involved in the hand to hand combat exercises. Hubert was observing a large German named Klaus, who was conducting the exercises.

Klaus was a tall, blonde haired, blue eyed, muscular Aryan. A pure killing machine, urged on by a true love for his work and zero tolerance for those who didn't or were incompetent. He stood in the middle of a small circle of men, towering over them.

Klaus looked over at Yusov and Hubert. Yusov nodded his head, signaling

Klaus, then turned to Hubert.

"Perhaps a demonstration," Yusov said to Hubert with a smile.

"Klaus called out to three men in the circle to attack him while Hubert watched. "Sergi. Luis. Garcia. It's your turn to try and chop down this tree."

The three men surrounded Klaus and moved in on him. They were all well built men of varying Hispanic backgrounds and knew that they had to go all out with Klaus or his wrath would be even greater than their easy defeat.

Klaus waited until they were all within striking distance before reacting. Sergi attacked first as he threw a punch at Klaus, who caught it in mid-air. His hand dwarfed Sergi's as he squeezed it. Luis and Garcia decided to move in on him together, but were also unsuccessful. Klaus, with lightning speed and dead on accuracy, immediately back kicked Luis in the chest with one foot and Garcia in the chest with a front kick, using his other foot. Both men fell backwards to the ground, landing with a heavy thud. Then Klaus pulled Sergi in toward him and punched him hard in the chest, knocking him off his feet and to the ground with another heavy thud.

Klaus just looked down in disgust at the three men sprawled out on the ground, trying to find the ability to breathe once more.

"Bravo. Bravo," Hubert said quite impressed as he clapped his hands.

"Klaus is my strongest man," Yusov said. "He's killed so many men, a cause of death should be named after him." Hubert smiled. Yusov was quite proud of himself for assembling such a crack unit of men for his mission. Most of them he had worked with before and some even against, but a common bond brought them all together. The common bond of professional survival— money.

"So, the accommodations are satisfactory, I take it?" Hubert asked confidently.

"Very. You've made all the arrangements with Santiago?" Yusov asked in return. Fernando Santiago was just a pawn in Yusov's plan, but a valuable one he needed. Hubert didn't know what those arrangements were and was acting only as a messenger. He would find out soon enough.

"Yes. Everything is set. He arrived shortly after you and has what you want on his yacht, The Natural Beauty. He will expect you around noon, tomorrow," Hubert answered knowing very little about what he was referring to. He knew Fernando Santiago was an arms dealer who dealt with terrorist groups like Black September and Red Jihad. Or anyone who could pay his price. "Good, when the time is right, he will be very useful," Yusov answered vaguely.

Demetri jogged over to Yusov from where the men were stretching out and doing general calisthenics. He wore the same khaki fatigues as all the other mercenaries, including Yusov.

"Comrade Yusov, I'm taking some of the men out for a run down the beach," Demetri informed Yusov.

"Good idea. I think I'll go with you," Yusov replied. He then turned his attention back to Hubert. "Governor, I hope you enjoyed your visit."

"It was very insightful. I'll see you for dinner at my place, tonight?" Hubert inquired.

Demetri signaled over to the ten men going for the run and they all started jogging in place next to Yusov and Hubert.

"Yes. I'll be there around eight," Yusov replied.

As Hubert got back in his BMW, Yusov and his men jogged by with Yusov on the side, keeping pace.

CHAPTER SEVEN

Halprin was napping peacefully while still reclining on the beach chair. The beach was mostly cleared off, with the exception of a few sunbathers and other stragglers. There was a silent calm in the air.

From the direction of the marina, Yusov and his men came jogging down the beach. They all ran in single file with Yusov on the side, keeping pace. As they moved down the beach, the volleyball net became an obstacle they would have to go around. Yusov directed his men up the beach to go around the net, rather than going down to the shore line.

Halprin was still napping in the beach chair, not as yet disturbed by the men approaching his position. As they started to pass by Halprin, Yusov was running in between him and his men and unintentionally kicked up some sand as he passed. The sand landed on the face of the already slightly stirring Halprin. He woke up and opened his eyes as he literally rubbed the sand from them and saw the last man in line pass before him.

Halprin sat up and was about to say something, but didn't as he turned his head towards the men rapidly moving away from him. His mouth gaped open as if to spill out some words, but none came out as he keyed in on Yusov's military trimmed, stark white hair. He stood up, still groggy from too much alcohol, and took a step toward Yusov, who was fading from sight. A look of déjà vu appeared on his face. He then just shook his head in disbelief trying to clear the cobwebs—there had to be a million guys with white hair. How often do you meet the object of a nightmare you haven't seen in thirty years and was probably long dead?

But then, Halprin's attention was distracted by a commotion coming from close by. The sounds of warning voices were from the marina not 100 yards away and took priority of Halprin's attention.

"Holy shit! She's coming in too fast!" one voice cried out, followed by another one. "It's going to crash into the marina! Get out of the way!"

Halprin started jogging down the beach toward the marina, picking up speed as he went.

Fifty yards out on the ocean water, the Treasure Seeker, a sixty-foot exploration boat, headed in toward the marina with a course heading and rate of speed that revealed the source of the panic coming from the boardwalk. The docking accommodations were placed according to size with the larger boats further out, but the Treasure Seeker was obviously way off course as it headed in toward where the smaller boats were docked.

Halprin could see the Treasure Seeker coming in as he ran up the beach. He leapt up the three short boardwalk steps and stood there for a moment to observe the situation. The people on the boardwalk were all scattering as impact became imminent.

Out on the small boat docks, a man in a speedboat was trying in vain to get it started and out of the path of the Treasure Seeker. The boat's engine refused to give in to the man's efforts, while back on the boardwalk his eight year old daughter was left standing alone. She cried out to her father while frozen in place by fear.

"Get out of the way daddy!"

The little girl's cries were either ignored or unheard by her father, but not by Halprin, who reacted to the calls for help. He also yelled out to the little girl's father, who was about to be crushed by the Treasure seeker, now only forty yards out.

"Get away from there! You don't have enough time!" Halprin called out loudly as he ran down the boardwalk.

The man on the speedboat looked over toward Halprin, whose warning yell caught his attention, then looked out at the Treasure Seeker and realized that he was indeed out of time. He tried to jump out the speedboat and onto the dock, but got tripped up when his foot got snagged in a docking rope. He landed on the dock with his legs still in the speedboat, entangled in the mess of rope.

With the Treasure Seeker less then thirty yards away, Halprin took off down the dock. He got down to the speedboat and jumped right in as the man was trying, unsuccessfully, to free himself. Halprin quickly managed to free the man's foot and helped him to his feet as the Treasure Seeker crashed into the docks.

Halprin and the man ran for the lives with the Treasure Seeker behind them, its size and bulk easily plowing through the docking lanes and the smaller boats, flinging debris into the air, wrecking the man's speedboat and a sailboat docked next to it.

As Halprin assisted the man down the dock with the Treasure Seeker gaining on them, the little girl stood frozen at the end of the dock where it met the boardwalk. Without a second to spare, Halprin scooped up the little girl and continued out onto the boardwalk. They jumped down to the soft sand on the other side of the boardwalk as the Treasure Seeker finally came to a stop with its bow sticking out over their heads.

The three of them were sprawled out on the sand, gazing up at the Treasure Seeker's bow. After seeing that the man and his daughter were all right, Halprin got up on his feet and looked up at the wreckage. He knew that someday he was going "buy" his way into the big soldier home in the sky, but I'll be damned he thought, nothing "naval" was going to send him there.

****

Kate and Joan had finished their lunch and were alerted to the collision by the commotion coming from the marina.

"What's going on down at the docks?" Joan said as she stood up to look around.

From where Kate and Joan were seated, they could not see the marina.

"I don't know," Kate replied as she too stood up.

They moved around to the street in front of the restaurant where they had an unobstructed view of the marina. On the other side of the street were more people from the hotel. Everyone gazed down toward the marina at the sight of the Treasure Seeker's collision with the dock and boats, looking like some mechanical beached whale.

"Oh, my God," Kate said, startled by what he saw.

Joan had a more pragmatic response. "Somebody screwed up--badly." Without even saying anything else to each other, Joan and Kate started down to the marina.

Parker and the rest of Halprin's men, except Walker, were among the bystanders from the hotel. They also headed down to the marina.

****

Halprin climbed up onto the boardwalk and was the only one near the Treasure Seeker. He walked over to the stern of the wreckage and peered into the boat. What he saw inside made him react quickly as he leapt up over the side of the boat in one quick motion to get a better look.

Landing on the deck, back near the stern, Halprin just shook his head at the carnage before him. Piled up in the corner of the boat near the front cabin were the dead bodies of the Treasure Seeker's crew, all chopped up by small arms fire. A blood trail led to the steering room cabin and Halprin cautiously followed it, being careful not to slip on the gory deck.

Inside the steering room cabin, a crewman was laid out over the controls with his hand clasped tightly around the throttle control, which still churned on. Halprin made his way over to the crewman and shut off the boat's engine.

The crewman came to and grasped for air as he slumped down in front of the control panel, facing Halprin with a horrified look on his face. Halprin, who had seen plenty of dead people, was shocked. He would have bet the crewman was dead. The guy obviously was not far from meeting the big admiral in the sky as his whole body shook in spasms as he continued to gasp for air. Halprin knelt down next to the dying crewman who suddenly clamped his hand down on Halprin's shoulder. With a bloody gurgling sound the dying crewman opened his mouth to force his words out.

"They came out of the sea."

The crewman coughed blood a few more times before finally dying.

Halprin slowly stood back up. He looked around the cabin and out through the boat's windshield and saw the people starting to gather around on the boardwalk. He didn't react to the swelling crowd until he saw the military uniforms worn by Kate and Joan, then he walked back out to the stern.

Kate and Joan made their way through the onlookers with Joan unapologetically leading the way.

"Make a hole! Coming through, here," Joan ordered the crowd.

"Excuse us. Military business," Kate said a little more courteously.

Kate's politeness was unnecessary due to Joan's formidable presence. Like a female John Wayne, the crowd parted willingly for Joan. They made their way up to the Treasure Seeker as Halprin was climbing down.

"Hey, who the hell are you and what do you think you're doing?" Joan yelled at Halprin, not at all pleased.

Halprin saluted Joan after taking in her rank, but wasn't apologetic with his response. "Caption Halprin, Special Forces. There's been some foul play here, Major. Since this is a U.S. registered vessel, I think you better take a look," he said confidently and self-assured as he looked back at the Treasure Seeker, then back at Joan. "I thought it would be a good idea to turn off the engine before it exploded any spilt fuel," Halprin finished as he spotted Parker and his men making their way through the crowd.

"I'm sure the locals appreciate your zeal, Captain, but you shouldn't trample to much on an apparent crime scene. The local authorities won't like it."   Joan said half-seriously.

Joan and Kate walked over to the boat's stern. The onlookers, still unaware of the massacre, were standing back about ten feet from the boat.

Halprin tried to ready them for what they were about to see as he noticed Kate for the first time, directing his caution toward her. "It's not pretty and appears to be a professional job. All double taps to the head with multiple rounds to the body for good measure--except the guy in the cabin."

Joan and Kate looked inside the boat and while Joan didn't express a reaction, Kate sucked in her breath as she put her hand over her mouth and turned her head away. Halprin tried to comfort her as he put a caring hand on her shoulder for a moment.

"It never is pretty, Captain," Joan said stoically. "As for it being professionals, that shouldn't be too much of a surprise, that's all we have around here."

Halprin looked back in the boat at the bodies, then out to the boardwalk as Parker and some of his men made it to the front of the crowd. Then back at Joan.

"I've already become aware of the criminal element around the island, but how often do they kill a boat full of American explorers?" Halprin asked cockily. "Doesn't seem like it would be good for business."

"No, Captain. It isn't," Joan replied. "And this never happens here in the Seychelles. You just don't kill Americans and get away with it. I promise you that."

"I take it you women are from the embassy and tracking station," Halprin deduced. "So I think you should know the guy inside the cabin was alive when I found him. He could only manage a few words before dying."

"I'm Caption Allen, this is Major Harris," Kate said as she made the introductions with piqued interest. "What did he say?"

"It didn't make much sense," he said. "They came out of the ocean," Halprin told Kate as he looked her in the eye. They were taken with each other. Instant chemistry.

Parker started to make his way forward to talk with Halprin.

"I'll have to ask you to stay back, sir," Joan said as she noticed Parker.

"This is Sergeant Major Parker. He is here with me along with my entire unit on leave," Halprin explained.

"Major, Captain," Parker said as he saluted both Joan and Kate, then shook their hands. Then he looked up at the Treasure Seeker and shook his head. "Can't leave you alone for a minute, huh, Jack. What happened? They cheat at cards?"

Halprin shook his head as he walked over to Parker and half whispered to him. "I think there's something more to this than a random killing."

"You mean they cheated the governor at cards?" Parker said as he smiled. "C'mon,

Jack. I'm sure the Major and the island authorities will be able to figure it all out, without our help. We're on leave, remember."

Halprin looked back at the boat, sensing Parker's reluctance to get involved, then at Kate and Joan. "If you need a statement or anything, I'm staying at the Hilton."

Joan just turned her attention back to the boat.

"Thank you, Captain," Kate responded to Halprin's offer by shaking his hand. "That would be great. You can reach me at the tracking station."

Halprin held her hand as the two prolonged the physical connection. Their eyes locked for a few seconds as they forgot themselves in the moment.

"Say, Jack. How 'bout you and I go get a drink at the hotel bar?" Parker said bringing Halprin back to reality.

Halprin let go of Kate's hand and turned to Parker. "Sounds like a good idea. I think I could use one about now."

The emergency crews made their way to the front of the crowd as Halprin and Parker started to leave.

"Captain Allen, I'd like to see you, again," Halprin said. "Do you think I could stop by the station to discuss a few things—say tomorrow afternoon."

"That would he just fine, Captain. I'll look forward to it," Kate said genuinely pleased.

Halprin followed Parker and his men back out through the crowd, passing by more emergency workers. As they reached the open boardwalk, Halprin noticed the Governor's BMW and Constable Moulin's official car pull up to the boardwalk and stop.

Halprin slowed down as he saw Hubert and Moulin stepping out of their cars. He arched his brow in curiosity as he locked eyes with Moulin.

Moulin was a swarthy, shrewd little man with a bug eyed look to him that suggested a distrustful nature just by his appearance. And in this case, the book could be judged by its cover. He was the second most powerful man on the island and head of the island police force, which consisted of six police cars and two dozen officers. Moulin was as corrupt as Hubert and would go to any lengths to get what he wanted.

CHAPTER EIGHT

Halprin and Parker sat at the end of a long rectangular bar that accommodated seating around its entire circumference. There were only a few other patrons seated at the bar and a few more at a nearby table. The lighting was low and the table's candles were lit for a more romantic atmosphere.

Walker was sitting at a table with Mara, the island girl he was so taken with earlier on the beach.

Four of Yusov's mercenaries, Klaus, Sergi, Luis and Garcia were seated at the opposite end of the bar from Halprin and Parker. They were accompanied by four island girls and all seemed to be having an affectionately good time.

Stella, the bartender, a voluptuous, dark haired woman in her late forties with a cigarette hanging from her heavily rouged lips was leaning back on the cash register when Halprin called to her.

"Say, beautiful. How about another round for me and my friend, here." Halprin drunkenly slapped Parker on the back to express his friendship toward his drinking buddy. Parker was also half in the bag, but had reached his limit as he put his hand over his shot glass. He smiled up at Stella causing the unlit cigar in his mouth to rise up with his drunken grin.

"I can always tell the customers had too much when they start calling me things like beautiful," Stella said in a heavy Texas drawl as she picked up a bottle of whiskey and walked over to Halprin and Parker.

"Now, I may have had too much to drink, but I always mean what I say," Halprin drunkenly declared.

Stella poured Halprin another shot and pulled out another beer bottle from the freezer underneath the bar.

"I'll just have another beer, darling. And I always mean what I say, too." Parker said as he waved off his shot, winking at Stella in a sly dog manner.

Stella winked back at Parker as she put down another beer in front of him while bending over the bar as her heaving breasts, barely held back from busting out of her by two tiny buttons, hovered there. She knew he was military from the way he spoke to the other man. That they had to be good friends, but were in disagreement about something. They both looked like they needed to relax. Didn't everybody?

"Well, I get off in about a half hour," Stella said still bending over in front of Parker. "Maybe you can help me get off in another way."

Parker was no old fool and felt her attraction toward him when he first sat down. And the feeling was mutual. Now, if only Halprin could start thinking about the pleasures of life instead of the painful aspects, he could relax and have some fun, too.

"Would be my pleasure," Parker said with a pleasing smile.

"You can count on it," Stella said before walking down to the other end of the bar where the mercenaries were calling for her services.

Halprin downed his shot then took a swig from his beer. He looked over at Parker as he propped himself up on the bar with his elbows.

"It's nice to see the old dog can still bark."

"You should be thinking about the same thing instead of what happened to that boat crew," Parker said as he lit the cigar he'd been chewing on.

"You have to admit that there's something strange about what happened out there," Halprin said expressing a more serious attitude.

"Even so. It's not your problem. I'm sure that Major Harris will find out exactly what happened, even if the island authorities are no help and inept."

"For a woman she certainly seems to have the balls for it. I'm going to pay a visit to the S.M.A.R.T. Station tomorrow, anyway. Just to check things out."

"You should forget about things that don't concern you. You're here to relax, remember. You were doing a pretty good job, too. Sleeping and everything," Parker stood up and stubbed out his cigar in an ashtray on the bar. "What you should do is go check out that sexy little Captain and have a good time. You deserve it."

Halprin smiled at the mention of Kate. "Oh, you don't have to worry about that. I definitely plan on seeing her."

"Good, stick to that plan and you'll be fine. Now, if you'll excuse me, I need to go have a word with this lovely lady."

Parker walked over to the middle of the bar where Stella was back by the cash register.

"Tell me your name, I'll give you my room number and I'll have them send up a late supper."

"Darling, my name is Stella and I'll be delighted to join you for supper, just don't order dessert. I'll bring that."

Parker placed his hand on top of hers as she leaned on the bar. As he did this, he caught sight of the mercenaries, still dressed in fatigues, at the end of the bar. They gave him a dirty look, but he didn't give them a second thought as he turned his attention back to Stella.

"Stella, I'm Sam. I'm in room two-o-five. Steak and lobster sound good?"

"Perfect. I'll be up in twenty minutes." Parker turned away as Stella went to get the mercenaries another round. Walker and Mara were sitting at a table nearby, holding each others hands while nose to nose in a kiss. Walker noticed Parker as they broke from their kiss.

"How is it going Sergeant Major?" Walker asked in a happy voice that carried out into the room.

Parker noticed as the mercenaries overheard Walker call him by rank. Walker also took note of this by their slight reaction to his words.

"Call me Sam. We are on vacation. No need for formalities."

Parker looked over at Halprin then back at Walker. "Keep an eye on Jack. Make sure he gets to his room all right."

"Sure thing," Walker said, understanding Parker's concerns. "I'm on top of it. You can count on me."

"Good man. You show this lady a nice time, now."

"Walker is a very special man," Mara said and kissed Walker then smiled up at Parker.

"Yes, he is."

Parker walked out of the bar and into the hotel lobby. He was thinking of starting supper with dessert.

CHAPTER NINE

Night had fallen on the island, the darkness temporarily covering all the events of the unusual day. A day that furthered the fears of Governor Hubert's decision to allow Yusov access to his island. But Hubert knew that Yusov and his sponsors could have just taken what they wanted at anytime. Not to say that Hubert's island was defenseless, but resistance would be futile against someone of Yusov's caliber or the might of his sponsor.

Hubert waited in the hallway entrance of his large white Victorian mansion, especially constructed just for him, as his butler greeted Yusov at the door. Hubert stood by the dining room doorway, looking nervous.

The butler walked Yusov up the hallway to Hubert, then disappeared down the hall. Hubert and Yusov entered the large dining room with a large dining table in the middle of the room, which was set for dinner for two—minus the food.

"I certainly hope that none of your men had anything to do with that nasty business today," Hubert said, as he walked over to the table. "That's the kind of thing that can cause all kinds of problems with the Americans."

"I assure you that all of my men on the island were accounted for. They'll probably just think that they stumbled upon some drug dealers hideout."

Just then, the butler and a maid returned each carrying dinner trays with silver covers on them, while the butler had a bottle of wine in his hand.

"Shall I pour the wine, sir?" the butler said after the setting down the dinner tray.

"No, that will be fine," Hubert said taking the bottle from the butler. "I'll get it. Leave us, now."

The butler and maid left as Hubert opened the wine. "I hope you brought a healthy appetite, Andrei. And a thirst for good wine."

Yusov walked up to the table as Hubert poured the wine. He lifted off the silver plate cover, revealing a sumptuous gourmet meal. "I always enjoy the opportunity to sit down to a good meal."

Hubert walked to the other end of the table as Yusov took a seat. He poured himself a glass of wine before sitting down and uncovering his meal.

"I don't know exactly what you are up to here on the island but you're paying me enough not to ask a lot of questions. I just want your assurance again that you won't interfere with the sovereignty of my country."

Yusov took a sip of wine before responding. "Excellent wine, Governor. And as I told you before, my mission here has very little, if anything, to do with the islands and I assure you no one will be able to connect us to you once we are gone."

"That makes me feel better, but that boat full of dead Americans is going to attract a lot of attention."

"The timing is unfortunate, but there are always unforeseen contingencies that one must be able to plan around," Yusov said taking a rather glib attitude towards Hubert's concerns about dead Americans.

"You sound like a man of great resolve," Hubert said as he took a sip of wine.

Yusov started in on his meal, enjoying the taste.

"That I am, Governor. Also one who appreciates the finer things in life."

"Bon appetit."

CHAPTER TEN

Vietnam 1968

There was total blackness. No light. No sound. Nothing. The world was no more. Existence was void.

Then there was sound. The sound of something moving. Brush breaking. But still total blackness.

Then there were voices calling out.

"You got anything over there?"

"Same as everywhere else. All dead and bloated."

"Keep looking. I know someone survived. I just know it,"

Light broke the blackness and slowly took form as viewed through the eyes of Jack Halprin as he lay buried under various enemy and friendly body parts, brush and dirt. The voice he heard caused him to come out of his subconscious state. It was a voice he had heard before. Then the moving feet of medical personnel and the body removal unit came into Halprin's field of vision. He could see the corpses of the dead being put into body bags and closed his eyes at the sight, bringing back the blackness.

"Look over there. What's that buried in the brush?"

Halprin opened his eyes at the sound of Parker's voice, bringing back the light.

Two feet of a medic walked right by Halprin's field of vision and continued past him.

"Nothing here, sir."

Parker's feet walked past Halprin, then stopped as he backed up and knelt down and his thirty years younger face came into Halprin's sight. Parker began throwing brush and battlefield debris aside.

"Medic! I got a live one!"

Parker yelled out as he lifted Halprin up from under the dirt and brush and as Halprin's vision cleared he found his voice.

"The devil has white hair," he muttered, as he drifted into unconsciousness.

****

Halprin woke up in his hotel room bed, repeating out loud the words from the dream.

"The devil has white hair. The devil has white hair."

He was lying on his stomach with his hand hanging off the side of the bed. He rolled onto his back and sat up in the bed. As he rubbed the sleep from his eyes, he saw Walker standing next to a chair across from the bed, by a little writing desk.

"You feeling okay, Cap?"

"Yeah, just fine." It took Halprin a few seconds to figure out that Walker was in the room. "Don't tell me Parker's got you watching over me."

"He was a little concerned with what happened yesterday."

"Well, I hope I didn't ruin your night with that cute, island girl."

"It's not like that," Walker said as he turned his head and blushed like a man falling in love, not lust. "Mara is a great girl and she works at her father's nightclub. The old guy is ill, so she's been closing up for him."

"Sounds like someone's in love," Halprin said as he put his feet on the floor and noticed that he was still wearing his pants.

"Yes, sir. I think I am," Walker declared as he snapped to attention to show his earnestness.

"That's great, Walker. I'm happy for you. I'd be even happier if I could remember how I got here."

"Ah, I kind of helped you along. I was just passing by this morning when I heard you call out."

Halprin got up and put on his shirt, not wanting to acknowledge Walker hearing him.

"If you don't mind me asking," Walker continued on even though he sensed Halprin's reluctance to talk about it. "What did you mean by the devil has white hair?"

"It is nothing," Halprin said with a sigh as he buttoned his shirt. "Just an old dream I keep having."

Then as if struck with a good idea, Halprin walked over to the door and looked outside in the hallway, then he moved closer to Walker.

"Walker, could you do me a favor?"

"Anything, Cap?" Walker said without even thinking about it. "You name it. If it wasn't for you, I don't know where I'd be now, except maybe in jail."

"You're a good man. The best in the unit. I've never seen anybody shoot like you. A kid off the streets of Philly who can take the eye out of a humming bird at five hundred yards. Hotdamn!"

"I learned from the best, sir."

"Don't let Parker know about this," Halprin said as put his hand on Walker's shoulder. "He'll just think I'm overreacting, but I want you to keep an eye on those mercenaries on the island. You've seen them, right?"

"There were a few in the bar last night and Mara told me they've been hanging around the nightclub. She said they were getting pretty rough with some of the girls."

"I don't want you starting anything with them," Halprin cautioned Walker. "Just watch them and see what they do. Then report back to me. Be discreet."

"You can count on me."

CHAPTER ELEVEN

Nine thousand miles away, in the White House Oval Office, Vice President Kimball sat behind the Presidential desk in a high black leather chair. He was leaning forward with his arms folded on the desk as he listened intently to his advisors presenting options on what to do about the situation in Iraq. They were being offered to him by the four heads of the military, along with the Secretary of Defense and several national security advisors. They all stood in front of the President's desk in a half circle around the White House Insignia on the floor.

Marine General Jack Roberts was voicing the strongest opinion on going for a full-scale military strike on Iraq.

"I feel the time is right to strike now, Mr. Vice President," General Robertson claimed.

"Our forces are ready and victory is most positively assured," Admiral Stewart Brown agreed. "There's never been a better time to take out Saddam."

Army General Nathan McCallister offered a different perspective. "As much as I would like to agree with my esteemed colleagues, I have to vote that we hold off, for now. It is true the polls are behind us, but if that video turns out to be fraudulent we'll be the ones with egg on our faces."

Secretary of Defense Walter Harvey agreed with General McCallister. "The U.N. Secretary General informs me that Saddam vehemently denies the ambush and has set up a meeting to discuss the monitored inspections of sensitive sites. Saddam claims he is being set up."

"Of course that's what he is going to say, but you can't believe him. He's lied before and he'll lie again. He's killed his own people with his lies!" General Robertson retorted.

Vice President Kimball leaned back in his chair to contemplate his options. His face remained expressionless so as to not reveal what he was thinking before it was said.

"Now, I know some of you are thinking how President Robbins would handle this situation and I'd bet most of you could make a pretty good guess, too. But I'm not going to sit here and think about what someone else might do."

Kimball stood up and walked around to the front of his desk and stood in front of it.

"I have to decide what is best for this country. What's best for the peace of the world at large. So, even though we are well within our rights to launch a military strike, I think it would be prudent to wait and see if a peaceful agreement can reached with the United Nations Security Council and proof of authenticity of that video tape. In any case, I can assure you gentlemen this, that there will be severe consequences to whomever is responsible for the death of those inspectors."

CHAPTER TWELVE

Two marines were stationed at the front gate of the S.M.A.R.T. Station and embassy. One was standing guard at the open iron gate, the other was inside the small guard booth attached to the entrance gate wall. It was late morning of a usual bright sunny day.

Halprin drove up to the S.M.A.R.T. Station in a rental car, a blue sedan with Island Rentals printed on the doors and back bumper. He pulled up to the front gate and stopped. The guard inside the booth came out with a clipboard in his hand and walked around to the driver's side of the car as Halprin rolled down his window and held up his identification.

"Captain Halprin, I believe I'm expected."

The guard looked down at the clipboard, then back at Halprin. "Yes, sir," he said as he saluted Halprin. "Go right ahead. I'll let them know you are coming. You can park inside on the right."

Halprin returned the salute as he drove through the gate. He parked in the visitor's section, got out, and walked over to the front entrance. He was dressed casually in slacks, a dress shirt, and a suit jacket.

Entering the front lobby, Halprin stopped and took note of the directory on the wall. The embassy was off to the right and down a hallway. Straight ahead was the S.M.A.R.T. Room and the cafeteria was to the left.

Kate came walking down the hallway directly in front of Halprin, coming from the S.M.A.R.T. Room. They were both genuinely pleased to see each other. She offered her hand as she reached Halprin, who shook it gingerly.

"Captain Halprin, it is nice to see you, again."

"Please, call me Jack. No need to stand on formalities. I am on leave."

"Okay, I'm Kate. How was your ride up here?"

"Just fine. I rented a car."

Kate was about to direct Halprin down the hallway to the S.M.A.R.T. Room when Colonel Vanderweel came walking towards them from the embassy hallway with Ambassador Harold Neville. Ambassador Neville was an older man with gray hair, around the same age as Vanderweel. They stopped by Kate and Halprin as Kate handled the introductions.

"Colonel Vanderweel, Ambassador Neville this is Captain Halprin. He was the first one on the scene of the Treasure Seeker tragedy. I'm also told that he saved the life of a man and his daughter," Kate finished while looking at Halprin, admiringly.

"You're a very brave man from what I understand, Captain Halprin," Ambassador Neville said as he shook his hand.

"Captain Halprin is a Special Forces unit leader. They're always on alert, even while on leave," Vanderweel added.

"I just happened to be there," Halprin said remaining humble, then inquisitive. "Have there been any further developments with the murders?"

"The local authorities are doing the autopsies on the crew and inventorying the crime scene later on today," Neville answered. "Major Harris is going down there to observe. Other than that, it's still a complete mystery. Who would do such a thing?"

"From what I've seen around the island, there's no lack of suspects," Halprin offered up.

Neville took up the role of a diplomat.

"We are well aware of the unsavory elements that frequent the islands and that Governor Hubert and the local police are corrupt, but it's also because of these factors that the island crime rate is almost nonexistent. Sure we have normal local problems, but nothing like this. Nobody around here wants to draw attention to themselves for obvious reasons."

"So whoever did this must have had a good reason," Halprin implied.

"Now we don't want to blow this out of proportion," Vanderweel said offering a different perspective. "This is probably an isolated incident and the Treasure Seeker crew was just in the wrong place at the wrong time. Tragic, but not conspiratorial."

"I think the Colonel might be right, which means it shouldn't take long to find out who is responsible," Kate agreed with Vanderweel just to move things along.

"Yes, Captain. I'm sure the killers will be caught and tried to the full extent of the law," Vanderweel said.

Kate turned her attention back to Halprin.

"If you're ready, Captain. I'll show you around the station, now," Kate said.

"By all means, carry on," Vanderweel said as he and Neville shook Halprin's hand again heading down to the cafeteria.

Kate led Halprin down the hallway and into the S.M.A.R.T. Room. A marvel of modern satellite communication capabilities.

"I didn't want to say anything in front of Colonel Vanderweel, but I also believe that there's something more to this than a random killing," Kate said as they walked through the S.M.A.R.T. Room.

Halprin slowed his pace as he became impressed by Kate's insight. She noticed this and waited for him to catch up as they walked past the long line of manned radar screens and communication consoles.

"You do agree with me, don't you?"

"Yes I do," Halprin said enthusiastically. "There have been too many strange occurrences happening in this region of the world at a highly volatile time. I'm just impressed by your perspective."

"Are you referring to the U.N. inspection team ambush? Because that doesn't make any sense to me."

"That is the problem with the world. Nothing makes sense anymore. Nobody trusts anybody. So no one believes a madman like Saddam when he says he didn't do it. Might as well cry wolf."

"I see what you mean," Kate said impressed with Halprin's point of view. "Saddam is the perfect target. Who'd believe him."

They reached the end of the communication consoles and Kate stopped at Specialist William's station. Williams turned around in his seat.

"This is Communication Specialist Williams. He intercepted a coded transmission, coming from Iran and directed out to one of the uninhabited islands, forty miles from here."

Halprin just arched a curious eyebrow as Kate explained further about the responding transmission.

"Twenty miles from the last reported position of the Treasure Seeker."

"Does the Colonel know about this?" Halprin asked more intrigued now.

"I told him, but he didn't think there was a connection. He is not the kind of man that acts on instincts."

"I know the type. Won't do anything without proof. Have you decoded the message, yet?"

Kate looked down at Williams, who took the cue to mean she wanted him to update her as well.

"Well, Captain. I'm still working on it, but other than it being a destination, the only other thing I can figure out is that it's an arrival time."

"A destination for what?" Halprin asked.

"I don't know what," Williams admitted. "I'm not even sure if it's a time of something coming or going. But whatever it is happens in about forty-eight hours. I just need more time to crack it. We don't usually pick up communications this far south from that region.

"Very good, Williams," Kate said praising his efforts. "Keep up the good the work."

"Do you have any maps?" Halprin asked Kate.

"Come into my office."

Halprin followed her to her office at the back of the room. They both entered the room and she headed over to the wall behind her desk where there were several maps hanging on the wall in a roll-up movie type set-up.

Halprin stood next to her as she rolled up the first map, which was of the main island, Mahe'. The second one was a map of all the islands of the Seychelles, she rolled that one up, too, revealing a third map of the Indian Ocean littoral.

They both looked up to Iran, while Kate ran her finger down the map, along the course of the transmission.

"Wait a second," Halprin said. "Lets go back to the map of the islands."

Kate pulled the map of the Seychelles down, which showed the layout of the islands.

"All right. Mahe' is right here," Halprin pointed out the island with his finger as Kate did the same with hers.

Their fingers touched for a second before Kate blushingly moved hers up to where the transmission went.

"Forty miles away is where the transmission went to," Kate explained the possible origin of the transmission and its destination.   Near this island, which has never been colonized, and is also, as legend goes, a suspected hiding place for buried pirate treasure."

"Just the kind of place an exploration boat might head," Halprin speculated.

"I checked the ship's manifest and that was their destination."

Kate and Halprin looked at each other in a shared moment of silent agreement. They both knew by their gut instincts that things weren't what they seemed and at that moment they formed a common bond, a common goal. Halprin had just assigned himself a new mission and Kate was going to help him.

"Kate, I don't know about you, but I believe there is a connection between all that is going on here. The transmission, the Treasure Seeker, and the U.N. inspection team ambush.   Someone is out there manipulating things and if someone doesn't do something it may be too late to stop it."

"Maybe if we both went to the Colonel again, he might listen to us," Kate suggested.

"Not without any proof," Halprin retorted as he walked away from the map. "He would just say we were paranoid."

"Well, Jack. Where do we start finding our proof?" Kate asked as she realized that he was right. It would be up to them to investigate this matter.

Halprin was pleased by Kate's willingness to help him, but he didn't want her to jeopardize her career. He was really starting to like her and he already did enough damage to his own career by being a maverick, which was why he was still only a Captain after thirty years of service. But the truth was that he wouldn't have it any other way. He didn't want a promotion, but Kate might have other plans and getting involved with him wouldn't be healthy for her career.

"Are you sure you want to get involved in this, Kate? It's the kind of thing that can ruin a career if we're wrong."

"If this is as big as you and I are starting to believe, I don't think I'll have to worry about that."

"All right, then. I guess it's up to us," Halprin said, with conviction. "I think we should take a good look at some of the local suspects. There seems to be a wide array of candidates."

"Hell, Governor Hubert would be a good place to start. He supplies training camps for mercenaries and sells fake passports. There is no real law here, even the local police force is under his control."

"Well, at least we can work together," she said with a twinkle in her eye.

CHAPTER THIRTEEN

The Mahe' General Hospital morgue was a typical cold, gray room where the presence of death was pervasive. Seven dead bodies of the Treasure Seeker crew were all laid out on separate examination tables, while the coroner, Dr. Phillips, stood over one of the bodies, about to conduct an autopsy.

A female assistant was there to hand him medical instruments. As he was about to begin, Joan walked into the room though two large swinging doors.

"Major Harris, glad you could join us. I was just about to start," Dr. Phillips informed her."

"I don't expect you'll find too many surprises," Joan said as a matter of fact.

"No.   It's pretty apparent that the others all died from bullet wounds, but this is the one who drove the boat into the docks," Dr. Phillips said with a slight mortician's laugh.   "Quite literally from what I hear."

Joan wasn't amused as she walked over to the examination table.   Dr. Phillips sensed this and decided to move on.   He spoke into a microphone attached to an overhead light as he recorded his findings.

"What we have here is a young Caucasian male between twenty-five and thirty years old.   Six feet tall and approximately one hundred eighty pounds. A slight contusion encompasses the front of the neck."

Dr. Phillips looked up from the body and called Joan over to point out the wound. "Here take a look, Major."

Joan walked around to Dr. Phillips side of the table as he lifted up the body to show her the entry wound.

"He was attacked from behind?" Joan said.

"Yes. Probably never even saw it coming. Point of entry indicates a big hunting or military type knife as the weapon. It appears to be the standard professional assault from behind, which would explain the contusion on the neck. Professional but sloppy."

"How so?" Joan wondered.

"Well, the knife didn't penetrate deep enough for the immediate kill. Suggesting that the killer was in a rush and did it in one quick motion."

"And the others?" Joan asked as she looked over at the six other corpses then back at Dr. Phillips.

"All standard execution style. I can only conclude that they were in a rush because they didn't sink the boat."

"Or they didn't want anyone investigating the area," Joan said offering her theory. "Thank you, doctor. You've been very helpful."

As Joan walked out of the room, she began to wonder if that Special Forces Captain might be right, but she also thought that there must be a simple explanation and not necessarily some big conspiracy.

CHAPTER FOURTEEN

The Paradise Nightclub was a cozy little place with several small cottages off to the side that served as overnight lodgings for the more amorous and intoxicated customers. A secluded location that was ideal both for midnight rendezvous and romantic excursions.

Due to the daytime hour, the parking lot was mostly empty.

Inside, the nightclub was also mostly empty with the exception of a few bar flies, discussing how they were once someone with real lives instead of spending their days and nights at the bottom of a bottle.

There was a large glittering disco ball hanging over the vacant dance floor and the empty tables—which still had their chairs on top of them from closing the night before—were also unoccupied.

The only other people in the bar were Walker and Mara. She stood behind the horseshoe bar with Walker sitting on a bar stool across from her. The entrance to the kitchen was located behind the bar.

"So, who is this other girl you're going to meet?" Mara teased Walker playfully.

"Now, you know I told you that I had to do some things for the Captain, today." Walker rationalized for her.

"You military men are all alike. Always following orders."

Walker leaned across the bar and took her hands in his as he looked deeply into her eyes.

"I'll see you later on, tonight. Then you can order me around all you want."

"You will be my love slave," Mara replied as they both laughed and kissed passionately.

When they broke from their kiss, Walker sat back on his stool.

"Damn, I think I'm falling in love."

"I know I am," Mara declared.

Walker was pleased to hear this, but then he changed subject while supporting a more serious look. "Have any of those mercenaries been around since the other night?"

"They are pigs!" Mara expressed her anger toward the mercenaries behavior. "When I got back last night after I left you, they were drunk and getting rough with some of the girls."

"Did they hurt anyone?" Walker asked as he started to look Mara over, almost as if he directed his question at her specifically.

Mara sensed this as she ran her hand though her long hair, pulling it in front of her shoulder, covering a small bruise there.

"No. No," Mara said as she quickly changed her attitude about the mercenaries. "They were just playing rough. The girls went along with them. Some of them stayed in the cottages last night."

Walker looked over at Mara's shoulder and reached his hand out, pushing her hair away from her shoulder.

"It is nothing. Really!" she insisted. "I told them I wasn't interested and they let me alone to tend bar while they partied with the other girls who liked them."

"Are they still there?"

"No," Mara answered quickly, thinking Walker would go after them. "They left this morning. I overhead one of them saying that they had to be down to the marina by this afternoon to meet somebody on a yacht."

"Did they say why? Hear any names?"

Mara thought for a moment. "The one I heard was called Klaus and from his attitude it sounded like they were meeting their leader. Someone called Yusov."

Walker didn't recognize Yusov's name.

"Did they say whose yacht?"

Mara closed her eyes as she tried to reflect back. "Santiago"

"Fernando Santiago?"

"That is all I heard. Do you know this man?"

"No. But I've heard of him," Walker said. Fernando was a well known arms dealer who always managed to avoid prosecution due to far reaching secret connections. "The Cap might be actually on to something."

Mara looked confused by all this.

"If any of those guys come back, stay away from them."

"Why? What is this all about?"

"I'm not sure. I just want you to know that no matter what happens, I'll always be there for you."

"I wish you wouldn't talk like that, you are scaring me, now," Mara said as she reached out and took Walker's hand in hers again.

"Don't be," Walker assured her. "It's nothing to worry about."

CHAPTER FIFTEEN

The marina and boardwalk were back in full swing again. The Treasure Seeker was still rammed though the docks and was blocked off with yellow police tape, but on the rest of the island it was business as usual.

Down on the other end of the marina where the bigger boats and yachts were docked along the boardwalk, the tourists, islanders and merchants were enjoying the sunny day. Walker was among the tourists, standing near a food stand, eating a hot-dog, trying to blend in while he watched three mercenaries walking down the boardwalk. Klaus was with Sergi and Luis. They stopped by the boardwalk's main entrance from the parking lot. They were wearing black fatigues and appeared to be waiting for someone.

They didn't have to wait long.

A Land Rover pulled in the parking lot in front of the boardwalk and stopped. Yusov and Demetri got out and walked up the boardwalk steps. They were casually dressed in plain clothes.

Walker finished his hot-dog and watch Yusov and his men as they walked over to a seventy-foot yacht with the name The Natural Beauty printed on the bow. Walker tried to look inconspicuous, but Yusov noticed him while walking up the boarding plank to the yacht.

Yusov looked right at Walker and could tell that he wasn't just gazing in his direction, this man had him and his men under surveillance. This bothered Yusov. This was not part of his plan, because he needed to meet with Santiago today. He would deal with this unwelcome observer later. There were more pertinent matters now.

As he reached the yacht at the end of the boarding plank, Yusov was greeted by Santiago who was a tall dark man who gave off a slime aura of someone who deals in guns. There were two armed body guards at his sides and more scattered throughout the yacht.

Klaus, Sergi, and Luis remained out on the deck, while Yusov and Demetri followed Santiago down below to the stateroom. In the stateroom were two more bodyguards and one of them was holding a gray suitcase. The stateroom also served as the control room from which the yacht could be run, aside from being a luxury lounge.

Santiago nodded to the man with the gray suitcase, and he handed it over to Santiago, who took it and put it down on a card table near Yusov.

"I certainly hope it was worth it," Santiago said slightly irritated and a little nervous. He didn't back away from the suitcase, but seemed cautious of it.

"Don't blame me for your carelessness," Yusov retorted. "Your men were incompetent."

"How were we supposed to know that an exploration boat would come by at the same time we were meeting with the sub to make a pickup?" Santiago said in his defense. "It could have jeopardized everything."

Santiago put his hand on top of the gray suitcase to illustrate this point. "And don't think I don't know what's inside."

"That is not your concern," Yusov replied firmly.

Santiago walked away from the suitcase a little more irritated with Yusov, but reluctant to express his displeasure further for fear of the repercussions. He was one of the few men alive who knew what

Yusov looked like. He had been supplying arms to him since the fall of the Soviet Union when Yusov went freelance, and it was always good business. He wasn't some cowboy, who'd be more trouble than he was worth, Yusov was a professional. The best at what he did. But this mission was different. Santiago saw it in Yusov's eyes. The "1,000 yard" look in them. Like he was looking through you. This was more than just another mission to Yusov and its successful completion held some deeper meaning that only Yusov knew.

"Even so, I don't like it. I'm going along with your plan because I'll stand to make a lot of money catering to both sides once the war breaks out, but I'm beginning to question your methods," Santiago carefully voiced his concerns.

"The suitcase is just a contingency plan," Yusov said. Nothing will be left to chance. But once we takeover the tracking station and scramble the satellite link, there will be no stopping us. They'll never know what hit them."

"Whoever is financing your mission, Andrei, must want to start a war with the United States and the rest of the world pretty bad."

"Who, what, or why doesn't matter. Only when," Yusov said philosophically. "The world needs this now more than ever. From chaos springs rebirth and it is time for man to be reborn."

Santiago didn't share Yusov's philosophy and kept his thoughts to himself as he walked over to a liquor cabinet and poured himself a drink. As far as he was concerned the only reason to do anything in this world was for gold.

"Care for a drink?" Santiago asked after he downed his first drink and poured himself another.

"No, thank you. We have to leave," Yusov said as he picked up the suitcase. "By tomorrow night, everything should be set."

"I hope so," Santiago said not quite as optimistically as Yusov. "They'll be watching things around here a lot closer now. This won't be a walk in the park."

"You must have faith, my friend."

****

Walker was still hanging out of the boardwalk in front of the yacht, when Yusov and his men came out. He started to slowly walk down along the merchandise stands and game booths, while keeping an eye cocked toward the yacht.

Yusov led the way back down the boardwalk with Demetri carrying the gray suitcase. Yusov noticed Walker for the second time as he made his way to the boardwalk steps. Klaus, Sergi and Luis left with Yusov and Demetri in the Land Rover.

After losing his quarry, Walker started heading towards the other end of the marina, down by the Treasure Seeker. As he reached the wreckage, he saw Halprin and Kate standing on the boardwalk, watching the salvage crew removing the Treasure Seeker from the dock. Halprin and Kate were facing the wreckage and didn't notice Walker as he came up from behind.

"Excuse me, Captain Halprin. You got a minute?"

Halprin and Kate turned at the sound of Walker's voice.

"Huh. Oh, yeah. Sure thing." Halprin said as he realized who was talking to him.

Before Walker could speak, Kate saw Joan pulling up to the boardwalk in an army jeep.

"Excuse me, Jack," Kate said sensing Walker's need for privacy.

"What did you find out?" Halprin asked.

"I don't know what they are up to, but I saw five mercenaries on a boat called The Natural Beauty."

"Fernando Santiago's yacht?" Halprin asked more as a statement of fact.

"That's right. They were only on it for a few minutes. But when they came off one of them was carrying a gray suitcase."

Halprin speculated what was in the suitcase as he let out a small sigh while looking at the Treasure Seeker, then back at Walker. "Catch any names?"

"Not from any of them. Mara told me they were hanging out at the nightclub last night and she overheard them saying where they were going. That's how I tracked them there. She said the three from the club were meeting someone called Yusov, who sounded like their leader, according to her."

Halprin wasn't familiar with the name, but as Walker described the mercenaries he said something that made things start to click.

"They all left in a Land Rover and I think one of them was this Yusov from the way they reacted around him. He had white hair, Captain."

"I'll be damned," Halprin said as he looked over to where Joan and Kate were talking as they started heading over.

"What do you think is going down, Captain?"

"I'm not sure, but I don't like the way things are starting to add up."

"I think they made me, too," Walker said softly as Kate and Joan made their way over. "The white haired guy noticed me as he was leaving."

This concerned Halprin.

"All right, then. Keep a low profile. Go hang out with your girl, tonight. You did well."

"What are you trying to do, Captain?"

"I don't know," Halprin said as Joan and Kate reached them.

"I'll catch up with you, later," Walker said, then saluted Joan and Kate before leaving. "Major, Captain."

As they returned the salute, Joan wondered what Walker was up to, before turning her attention to Halprin.

"Well, Captain. I see you have the penchant for playing Sherlock Holmes and seem to have inducted Captain Allen to be your Dr. Watson."

"It is not like that, Joan," Kate interjected. "I agree with Jack. There is something going down and this island seems to be at the center of it all."

"That's all right, Kate, I'm not going to try and stop you," Joan said. She didn't shoot down Kate's theory, or fully support it, either. Letting these two nose around was the best way to find some answers without causing any public relations problems. She knew Kate to be a stable, intelligent individual who wouldn't go off half cocked, but this Captain Halprin was different. "If you come up with anything substantial, how about bringing it to me first before doing anything. Let's save any foolish heroics until we all can be involved, Captain Halprin. I know how you Special Forces guys can get."

Halprin smiled along with Kate, feeling that they've won over Joan.

"You have my word, Major," Halprin assured her.

"Very good, Captain. I'll hold you to it," then to Kate. "I'm going back to the station, want a ride."

Kate looked at Halprin, who felt inclined to answer for her.

"I was hoping Kate would join me for dinner."

"I would like that very much," Kate said having no problem answering for herself this time.

"Very well, then. I'm sure Kate will fill you in on the autopsy report, Captain." Joan said before walking away, leaving Kate and Halprin standing on the boardwalk.

"So, where's a good place to eat?"

CHAPTER SIXTEEN

"I don't see him anywhere."

"Me neither."

Three mercenaries stood in the entrance way of the Paradise Nightclub. Klaus, Sergi, and Luis were scanning the packed bar and crowded dance floor as the night began to come alive.

Mara was tending bar, along with two other girls, and didn't notice the three mercenaries walk in. Klaus looked over at her, remembering her from the night before in both the hotel bar and here later on that night. She was the one they were looking for, the friend of the one Yusov pointed out to him on the boardwalk. The one who was watching them.

"He'll show up to see his bitch," Klaus said as a sadistic smile crossed his face, while nodding towards Mara.

"That's her behind the bar. The one from the hotel. She was getting quite cozy with him."

She's the one he was with when he called that old guy Sergeant Major," Luis pointed out.

"Yusov was right. He's military," Klaus concluded.

"So, what's he doing here?" Luis wanted to know.

"Probably just on leave," Klaus figured. "But he wasn't on the boardwalk this afternoon by chance. He had us under surveillance."

"You want to wait and see if he shows?" Sergi asked.

"I got a better idea," Klaus said as he concentrated his eyes on Mara. "Lets bring him to us."

Klaus started over to the bar, and Luis and Sergi looked at each other as they nodded their heads, understanding Klaus' unspoken plan, before following.

Mara was busy with a customer and didn't notice Klaus walk over to the end of the bar where the kitchen was located. Nor did she see him flip up the bar top entrance gate as he slipped quickly behind the bar.

Luis and Sergi remained on the other side of the bar as they encouraged a young couple to move from their seats, next to the bar top entrance. The young couple, honeymooners from France, relinquished their seats willingly, without a word, realizing just from the mercenaries' facial expressions that staying would be unhealthy.

Mara turned her attention toward the kitchen and saw the young couple walking away as Luis and Sergi took their seats. She frowned at the sight of the mercenaries and Klaus standing behind the bar, but she put on a false smile as she went over to take their order.

"What can I get you, gentlemen?" Mara asked as she bravely walked right up to Klaus, unaware of the impending danger. She played it friendly as she pulled up a bottle of whiskey and three shot glasses. She then filled them while at the same time tried to gently nudge Klaus back around to the other side of the bar.

"You look like whiskey men. How 'bout I just leave you the bottle on the house," Mara offered as she moved closer to Klaus, which was just what he wanted.

Klaus reached around behind his back and retrieved a knife from a sheath attached to his belt. Holding the knife down low by his side, he held his ground as Mara gently placed his hand on his shoulder in an effort to get him to step back. But Klaus wouldn't give ground.

"All I ask is that you stay on the other side of the bar, please," Mara persisted, still trying to urge Klaus to back out.

"That just won't do," Klaus said as he brought up the knife and pressed the tip of the blade under her rib cage.

Mara instinctively recoiled backwards, but Klaus put his free hand on her shoulder and pulled her to him as he whispered in her ear.

"Move or cry out and I'll gut you like a fish, right here behind the bar," Klaus threatened, as his hot breath penetrated her ear, making her shiver.

"I won't," she replied in a calm voice as she tried to mask her fear, but her body trembled slightly.

"Smart girl. Now let's move into the back," Klaus said, as he looked toward the kitchen, which appeared closed and empty.

Mara quickly scanned the room with her eyes, without moving her head, in a desperate attempt to see if anyone could help. Klaus smiled sadistically as he noticed Mara's darting eyes.

"Don't worry, I'm sure your soldier boy will show up," Klaus teased her while still breathing his hot breath in her ear. "In fact, I'm counting on it. Now move, bitch."

Mara realized that she was out of options at the moment and did as instructed. Klaus stayed close by her side, keeping an arm around her waist, suggesting that they were a couple, as he kept the knife pressed firmly up against her ribs while they walked into the kitchen.

Luis and Sergi followed them as they all exited the bar unnoticed in the ruckus.

The kitchen had been shut down since Mara's father had taken ill. He was a world class chef and the kitchen was his domain. The nightclub was originally a restaurant but as tourism boomed on the island Governor Hubert kept raising taxes, which forced him to find a more profitable business or face losing the place. This broke the old man's spirit, but he was still able to provide for his family.

Mara could still feel her father's spirit as she walked through the abandoned kitchen, even as Klaus pushed her through the room.   Everything was clean and in perfect order, pots and pans hung from overhead racks, casting shadows on the ovens and stoves.

"Where are you taking me? What do you want with Walker?"   Mara asked defiantly finding courage from the power of her father's spirit. She spotted out a wood block carving knife holder at the end of a preparation counter about three feet in front of her.

Klaus tightened his grip on her arm as he could sense Mara's desperation.

"I'll ask the questions, bitch. Just keep moving out back and don't even think about it," Klaus said as he pushed her past the knives on the counter.

Luis and Sergi followed behind, amused by Mara's bravery as they laughed snidely. The back door of the kitchen loading dock swung open as Klaus shoved Mara out of the building and into the night air. There was a large dumpster set up next to the loading dock. They all moved down the steps with the only sounds being the scurrying of a rodent, chased down and caught by a cat. The irony of nature wasn't lost on Mara's predators.

Luis imitated the sound of the cat's snarling screech as it tackled its prey, causing Sergi to do likewise. Klaus wasn't amused even though it was frightening Mara.

"You two better shut the fuck up and screw your heads on before I shove them up your ass," Klaus said as he stopped in his track and turned around to face them, while still keeping a firm grip on Mara's arm.

Luis and Sergi became serious quickly.

Klaus led Mara by the arm as he headed for the cottages. He settled on the first one, which was dark inside and unoccupied. Mara pulled back in fear as she realized where they were taking her, but Klaus just pushed her up the steps and into the front door of the cottage. She banged off the door, but was quickly pressed back up against it as Klaus stepped up close behind her.

"Don't mess with me, bitch," Klaus said as he ran his hand up along the outside of her thigh and over her buttock before finding the door knob. Pushing the door open, he shoved her inside.

Mara stumbled into the cottage, but managed to keep her balance and stay on her feet. There was a bed directly in front of her, along with other furniture spread out in the cottage. She turned around as Klaus, Luis, and Sergi walked in.

Luis turned on a light on a dresser next to the door.

"I want you to tell me everything you know about your soldier boy, starting with why he was following us?" Klaus asked as he put his knife away, having trapped his prey.

"I have no idea what you're talking about," Mara said as she sucked in her breath, trying to remain strong.

Klaus looked over to Luis and Sergi, standing at his sides, then back at Mara.

"I like you. You got guts," he said with a falsely pleasing smile. "That is rare in a woman. No brains, but guts." Then without warning, Klaus backhanded her across the face, sending her flying backwards. She lost her balance this time and fell back on the bed.

Klaus stood over her as Luis and Sergi moved in and formed a human wall. "You are going to tell me what I want to know or...hell, first things first," Klaus said, as he knelt down while undoing his pants.

Mara just shivered in fear as he moved on top of her, ripping her blouse open and exposing her firm, young breasts. His hot breath now moved down on her lips where the taste made her feel sick as he licked her face like a dog.

CHAPTER SEVENTEEN

Halprin and Kate sat at a cozy, candle lit table in the Chez T'ed restaurant. Having just finished their dinner, they settled back sipping wine while getting to know each other better.

"So, Kate. Why did you choose to come to the islands? I'm sure you had a wide choice of posts to pick from."

"I was just about to ask you the same thing," Kate said with an ironic smile.

Halprin hesitated for a moment before answering, reluctant to answer his own question. "I asked first."

"Okay," Kate said giving in easily. "Umm. I'm not really sure," she had never really given it much thought before and she found it amusing to think about now. "I grew up in a small town in New Jersey and I never traveled anywhere. I always wanted to see the world, which is why I joined the Air Force. The island sounded like something out of a fantasy novel, so I thought it would be different. Going someplace that I had never heard of, that hardly anybody even knew existed."

Halprin thought about the anonymity of the islands for a second, logging it into his memory, while still paying close attention to Kate.

"It has been a great experience here, aside from the Treasure Seeker tragedy that is, but even that has a positive side."

"It's a lousy way to meet someone, but that's just one of the many strange ironies of life," Halprin said sincerely.

Kate liked Halprin's philosophic outlook as she sipped her wine and nodded her head.

"So, Jack. What made you choose the island? You don't seem like the kind of man who'd be relaxing on a beach. Then again, you don't seem like the kind of man who relaxes much at all."

Halprin was once again impressed by Kate's perceptiveness. She was a smart woman who could see past the surface of things which was where real truth usually hid.

"You're right. It wasn't exactly my idea to come here, but I'm glad I did, especially under the present circumstances," Kate blushed as she took it as a compliment. Halprin continued. "My friends plus a few higher ups recommended that I go on leave. They were under the impression that I was overworked."

"Were   you?"   Kate   asked   truly concerned. "I mean, you sound like you didn't agree with them."

Kate leaned forward and reached her hand across the table, placing it on top of

Halprin's in a comforting gesture. "I can tell there is something driving you, and I want you to know that you can confide in me."

Halprin turned his hand up to hold hers in a show of appreciation for her compassion. He let go, though, as he sat back to bare his soul.

"For the past thirty years, I've been having this recurring nightmare from the time my brother was killed in Nam, during the Tet Offensive. I was on patrol with him, and was almost killed myself."

"Oh, my God. That must have been awful," Kate interrupted as she expressed her sympathy.

"I always thought that the dream meant something," Halprin continued. "That I wouldn't subconsciously fixate on it unless it was important. Up until now, I thought it was because I felt I could have done something to save my brother, and the only way to deal with it was if I kept moving. So I took every assignment I could get, never wanting to stop, always moving so my mind wouldn't have time to drag me back into the nightmare."

Halprin pushed his chair back in frustration of revealing his personal demons. "Look, I don't even know why I'm telling you this. I never told anyone about the dream and its effect on me until now."

"Why now? You look like it has affected you even more than normal," Kate asked sensing some deeper secret.

Halprin moved his chair back in as he leaned forward not wanting anyone to overhear their conversation. "This is going to sound crazy, but during the firefight— hell, slaughter when my brother was killed, I saw a white man with stark white hair leading the North Vietnamese. I'll never forget it. His face was just a blur as I sighted through my rifle scope, but before I could shoot an air strike came and it was lights out. That was the last thing I remember. Over the years I don't even know if the white-haired guy that day was a product of my imagination or not. Then yesterday, just before the Treasure Seeker crashed, I thought I saw the same white-haired bastard leading the mercenary group for a run down the beach, but I only got a glimpse of him from behind. Hell, I can't tell you the number of white-haired guys I've seen over the years that I thought was the man. But this time is different. I somehow know it's the same guy. I also have a sick feeling that he has something to do with what's happening and that this is only the beginning."

Kate listened intently to what Halprin said and seemed to be agreeing with him with her eyes alone.

"What can we do?"

"I'm not sure," Halprin admitted. "Can't go to the Colonel without any proof. Parker already thinks I'm overreacting, and he knows that I'll want to confront this guy on my own terms. Unfortunately, the only thing we can do now is to be prepared to move quickly when something breaks and hope it's not too late. This island is part of it, though, that much I'm sure of. The answers are right here. We just have to ask the right questions and hope no more bodies turn up."

CHAPTER EIGHTEEN

Walker jogged down the narrow lane road leading to the Paradise Nightclub. He had fallen asleep back at the hotel and slept longer than he wanted, but it was a clear, calm night and the nightclub was only a couple of miles away, just perfect for an evening run. The trip also gave him time to think as the night air woke him up. He wanted to give some serious thought to his strong feelings for Mara, and the run was the perfect way to clear his head. This girl he only knew a couple of days consumed his mind in a way no other had before. There were plenty of women in his life, but never anyone serious. In high school he had his pick, with his good down-home looks and his charming sincerity. But now he knew he wanted somebody other than some ditzy cheerleader or stuck up snob.

The Paradise Nightclub appeared before Walker as he rounded a bend in the road, and it was at that moment that he decided to ask Mara to marry him. He wanted to spend the rest of his life with her, even if he had to resign from the army. The army had been his life for the past eight years, and Captain Halprin was like a father to him, but his feelings for Mara went beyond all that. She was the one for him. He knew that now, and he wasn't going to let his chance at true happiness pass him by like it had for so many other military men in his position.

Being in peak physical shape, Walker's breathing was normal as he jogged up to the Paradise and stopped at the front steps. He momentarily rested so he could get the words just right in his head. He would have to explain to Mara how he couldn't leave until he was sure Captain Halprin was okay with the situation. There was something very suspicious about the mercenaries meeting with Santiago, but there would be time to think about that later, now he had to sum up another kind of bravery. The bravery of expressing his love, of giving his heart to someone, of wanting to share his life with that person. It was going to take as much courage for him to talk to Mara as it would be to get shot at.

The crowd inside the Paradise had thinned out somewhat since Mara's abduction, which had gone unnoticed. The music and dance floor were still going strong, but the bar was less packed then before.

Klaus was waiting like some fierce predator, sitting by himself at a table in a darkened corner of the club. He knew he wouldn't have to wait long, and recognized Walker as he entered the nightclub. Klaus didn't move as he continued to wait to see what his quarry would do.

Walker stood in the doorway, looking around for Mara. He walked over to the bar and up to Lorna, one of the other two bartenders, after not seeing Mara anywhere.

Lorna, a tall, thin blonde, was busy with another customer as Walker reached the rail. She knew Walker especially the way Mara kept talking about what a good man he was, and that she had strong feelings for him. She gave him a big friendly smile of someone who knew something good about that person and that they were about to find out what, just not from her.

"Hey, Lorna. How's it going? Have you seen Mara? I was supposed to meet her here, but I overslept."

"I haven't seen her for awhile," Lorna said looking around as she noticed for the first time that Mara wasn't there. "Maybe she's taking a nap in one of the cottages."

"Any idea which one?"

"They're all full except for the first one. That one is always empty."

"Thanks," Walker said as he headed back out of the nightclub with Klaus' eyes following him all the way.

Walker left the bar and headed right over to the first cottage, which was dark inside. Once there, he opened the door, peered inside, and called out to Mara.

"Mara, honey. Are you in here?"

Walker reached inside the door and felt around for a light. Stepping inside the cottage as he located the light on the dresser, he tried to turn it on, but there was no light. Then Walker heard muffled sounds coming from the bed as he walked over.

"Mara is that you?"

As he got to the bed, all he could make out was a shadowy figure struggling on the bed. Then the room was flooded in light as Luis turned on another lamp by a card table. Walker didn't see Luis or even care where the light came from at first as his eyes were fixed on the sight of Mara tied to the bed and gagged. She had been beaten, her eyes already darkening to black masses, lips bruised and bloody, her blouse almost completely torn away revealing more bruises on her shoulders and breasts. Her skirt was torn up to her crotch but the real horror lay in her fear filled eyes, which knew the worst wasn't over and had only just begun.

"Hey, shithead."

As Walker turned his head toward the voice, he was greeted by Luis' fist being slammed into his face. He stumbled back into the arms of Sergi, who grabbed him from behind and held him there for Luis to hit.

Luis slammed his fists into Walker's stomach several times, causing Walker to seemly weaken and slump to the floor as Sergi no longer felt the need to hold him up.

"I told you these Special Forces boys weren't that tough," Luis bragged quite proud of himself.

"A bunch of women," Sergi quipped.

Luis and Sergi laughed at their premature victory only to be cut short by Walker grabbing hold of both of their genitals. He squeezed tightly as he pulled down, bringing them both to their knees screaming in a helpless state of pain.

"You two assholes are about to become women. But first you're going to tell me what the fuck you're doing here."

Walker tightened his grip as both men squirmed in pain, but remained silent. After sensing their unwillingness to talk, even under the extreme circumstances, Mara's need for aid induced Walker to let go of Sergi's genitals and quickly punched Luis in the face. Then as Luis fell backwards, Walker caught Sergi with an upper cut that sent him sprawling backwards on the floor.

Walker quickly got on his feet, but this time, Klaus was there to great him as he stood in the doorway and kicked Walker in the chest, sending him flying backwards, landing on top of Mara.

"Get up you dogs!" Klaus ordered as he looked down at Luis and Sergi in disgust.

As Walker quickly regained his composure, he got off Mara and went after Klaus. He threw a punch at Klaus, who caught it in mid air.

Klaus stood a foot taller than Walker and began to crush Walker's hand in his. Walker tried to throw his other fist at Klaus, but he caught that one too, and slowly forced Walker to his knees. Once he had Walker at his mercy, Klaus kneed him under the chin, sending him falling to the floor, unconscious.

Klaus went over and quickly bound Walker's hands behind his back, using a plastic zip tie from his pants pocket. He rolled Walker on his back as he started to regain consciousness.

Walker's dog tags were visible as they hung out from under his shirt collar. Klaus reached down and yanked them off.

"Get him on his feet if you think you can manage that," Klaus said as he turned to Sergi and Luis, who were still holding themselves in pain. His look of disgust for them had not faded.

Luis and Sergi did as they were ordered and stood Walker up and held him in place. Klaus stood in front of him face to face. He held the dog tags for Walker to see as he reached behind his neck with his free hand.

"This should give your friends something to keep them busy and out of our business," Klaus threatened.

Walker spit in Klaus' face, disdainful of what repercussion might come. But Klaus didn't wipe the spit away. Instead he just smiled sadistically at Walker.

"You are going to be real sorry you did that," Klaus said as he whipped out his knife from behind his back and held it to Walker's throat. He then pressed the blade against the flesh, causing a small trickle of blood to run down his neck. "Real sorry."

Klaus suddenly spun around and came up on the other side of the bed where Mara was tied, helplessly. In one quick motion while looking Walker directly in the eye, he slit her throat open, causing her whole chest and neck to turn red as the blood flowed out in a stream.

"Noooo!" Walker cried out as he struggled to break free, but Luis and Sergi punched him in the back and ribs, causing him to fall to his knees.

Walker's eyes welled up with tears as he felt the pain of loss more than the physical punishment.

CHAPTER NINETEEN

Halprin and Kate stood on the sidewalk in front of the Chez T'ed restaurant. The street was empty and they had the night to themselves. It was that awkward moment at the end of a first date when you don't know what to say.

"Good meal, great company," Halprin said to break the silence that was building.

"It's been a lovely evening, Jack. Thanks." Kate said relieved that he spoke first. "I think we both needed this, after everything that's happened. Maybe in the morning we will have a fresh perspective."

"I guess I should be getting you back to the station." Halprin said while looking at his watch, thinking that Kate might want to go.

"Jack," Kate said in a soft seductive voice realizing that Halprin didn't get her subtle innuendo. "I don't want to have to go back, and I really don't feel like being alone tonight."

Halprin took her hand in his and held it gingerly while looking deeply into her eyes. "I don't want to be alone tonight, either."

Halprin pulled her close and they locked into a passionate kiss, letting their emotions run wild, uninhibited by their surroundings.

****

The door to Halprin's hotel flew open from the weight of Halprin's and Kate's bodies pressed against it as they moved into the room still embraced in a passionate kiss.

Halprin kicked the door shut with his foot as they moved over and collapsed on the bed. They started to remove each others clothes while positioning themselves on the bed. First they kicked off their shoes, while unbuttoning each others shirts. Halprin cupped his hands over Kate's firm breasts, still enclosed in her white bra, while she unbuttoned his pants and slid them down to his waist. He removed her bra and Kate let out a pleasurable moan as Halprin started kissing her breasts. Then he slowly worked his way down her body, kissing her belly while removing her skirt and panties. He pulled himself on top of her naked body and put his lips on hers, once more as their passion ran wild.

Halprin's hotel room window had a view of the marina, with the moonlight shining off the water, reflecting the light in the room while they made love. Halprin's life in paradise was copacetic.

CHAPTER TWENTY

It was only a few hours before dawn and all was quiet on the boardwalk and in the marina. A drunken vagrant was sleeping on a dilapidated bench, about twenty feet down from Santiago's yacht. His empty wine bottle next to him.

Yusov's Land Rover pulled into the parking lot in front of the main access to the boardwalk. He stepped out accompanied by Klaus, Luis, Sergi, and also Walker—who was unconscious and helped along by Sergi and Luis. They followed Yusov and Klaus up the boardwalk steps, dragging Walker with them.

The drunken vagrant, disturbed by the sound of Walker's dragging feet, lifted his head and watched four shadowy figures with two dragging a fifth up the boarding plank of Santiago's yacht. Sitting up on the bench while scratching his privates, the drunken vagrant reached down for his bottle as Yusov and his men boarded the yacht.

"It's getting so a man can't get any sleep around here," the drunken vagrant mumbled as he located the empty bottle and tried to suck one last drop from it. After not being able to extract anymore of the precious liquid, he got to his feet and staggered there a moment then sat back down. He was about to lay down again when he was disturbed once more by a sound in the night.

The roar of a speedboat engine coming from Santiago's yacht rang out in the marina, causing the drunken vagrant to get to his feet again. He saw the speedboat leaving as it pulled out from the yacht and headed out into the ocean.

****

An hour later, the speedboat was stopped and floating on the calm ocean water with an uninhabited island in the background, about two hundred yards away.

The situation was desperate for Walker as he hung from an engine winch over the deck of the speedboat. His hands were bound above his head and hooked onto the winch. He had been badly beaten and sported large welts on his face, bare chest, and ribs. His feet were also bound together. To make matters worse, Luis and Sergi took turns taunting and beating Walker as he hung helplessly.

"So, who is a woman, now, bitch?" Sergi said as he slammed his fist into Walker's defenseless body.

"You are going to scream like a woman, very soon." Luis taunted, making the mistake of getting too close to Walker.

Walker managed to lift his bound feet and kick Luis in the face causing him to fall backwards and practically overboard.

"You broke my fucking nose, you bastard," Luis cried with blood dripping down on his face. He quickly got up and charged Walker, but was literally pulled off his feet and thrown back to the deck as Klaus clamped a hand on his shoulder and forced him down.

"Still thinking with your asshole, I see," Klaus chastised Luis.

Yusov walked over from the small the steering cabin. Luis got to his feet and stood at attention while Yusov just shook his head. He spoke while facing Luis, but turned and faced Walker as he finished.

"You should never underestimate your enemy. Always believe in his abilities and determination to live. That way he will never surprise you."

"I don't know what you're up to, but it's not going to happen the way you want," Walker informed Yusov.

"That is something you are not going to have to worry about," Yusov said while staring down Walker, keeping his distance.

Yusov nodded to Klaus, who swung Walker out over the side of the boat where he hung a few feet above the water.

"What you do have to worry about is how painfully you are going to die," Yusov suggested. "Tell me what I want to know and I'll put a bullet in your head and get it over with quickly, otherwise, I'll make you bleed and feed you to the sharks."

Walker didn't say anything right away as he contemplated his dire position. Yusov seemed to sense his hesitation and decided to fill him in on what was already known.

"I'll save you the feeling that you betrayed your comrades by telling you that your bitch already told us that you're part of twelve man Special Forces unit here on leave. But what I don't understand is why you had us under surveillance. Were you acting under orders or did you just get a bug up your ass over that girl? Tell me!"

What the hell Walker thought. Go for broke.

"I'll make you a deal. I'll tell you all I know if you tell me what you're up to," Walker insincerely proposed to Yusov, knowing he didn't have much time.

"All right," Yusov said smiling at Walker. "But make no mistake, you are going to die here. This is not one of your American movies where the bad guys reveal their plans to the good guy moments before he makes a daring escape. And I am the main bad guy," Yusov boasted.

"So, what do you have to lose, asshole," Walker retorted, managing a smile through broken teeth.

Luis started to throw bait overboard to attract the sharks and smiled up at Walker, sadistically.

"The American people have enjoyed the freedom from responsibility for their economic stranglehold on the world for too long."

Yusov grimaced in a stone cold expression of hate as he felt an illogical need to tell someone his plan, and who better than an enemy who was soon to die. "After tomorrow night, that will all change. The rest of the world will turn against the United States of deception for starting a war for the sole purpose of preventing the United Nations from lifting the sanctions imposed on Iraq. Especially, considering that since the inspection team ambush, Saddam is about to cut a deal to allow inspections because he knows he's being set up."

"He just doesn't know by whom."

"They never do."

"So, how are you going to start this war?"

"You just won't be happy until you know, will you?"

"Let me die happy," Walker said laughing off his own impending death.

"Okay, then.   After I take over the S.M.A.R.T. Station and shut down the satellite link, a nuclear submarine hidden out there somewhere..."   Yusov waved his hand out over the water.   "Will launch a warhead at Baghdad making it look like the U.S.S. Nimitz did it.   So now, why were you following my men?   Was it because of that whore or were you acting under orders?

Luis stood up from throwing the bait overboard and had a large fish gutting knife in his hand.   "I think it is feeding time."

Walker looked down at the clear water and could see several shark fins circling in the water directly beneath his feet.

"I'll tell you what this American knows," Walker said while keeping a cool smile aimed defiantly at Yusov. "You are going to die hard, motherfucker."

"And you're shark food," Yusov laughed off Walker's attempt to anger him. Then he turned to Luis and Sergi. "Do it!"

Luis moved in first and reached out with his knife and sliced it across Walker's rib cage. A small trickle of blood formed and dripped into the water.

"I'm going to tenderize you real good for breaking my nose," Luis threatened, but foolishly turned his head for a second to look back at Sergi to gloat.

Walker, once again, swung himself up in the air by doing a pull up on the winch. He raised his legs above Luis' head, bringing them down around his neck this time as he twisted himself off the winch hook.

Walker fell into the water dragging Luis with him. They both landed with a big splash as everyone on the boat was surprised by Walker's ballsy move.

The two men sank down into the ocean depths as the sharks began to seek their prey. Walker knew that if he could wrestle the knife out of Luis's hand he might have a chance. Hell, pigs might fly to. Just then the only thing he wished for was to live long enough to avenge Mara.

Yusov, Klaus and Sergi all gazed over the side of the speedboat as blood stained the water around the boat.

"Like I said, never underestimate your enemy," Yusov repeated.

"Least he's dead. I'll worry about him when I get to hell," Klaus said.

CHAPTER TWENTY-ONE

Back in Washington, D.C., Vice President Kimball was not about to underestimate his unknown adversary, either, or he would wind up being eaten by the political sharks who were just waiting for him to screw up. Kimball had always envisioned himself as succeeding President Robbins—who was two years into his second term when a tragic accident put him in a coma—but not like this. He wanted to be the man in charge of the country in the new millennium. It would be one of the most significant times in history, a jumping off point for new beginnings, new policies, a new outlook that he would implement to help bring peace and harmony to a world in turmoil. He knew that there was a strong fear globally that the world would end in the year 2000—or soon thereafter. When it didn't, then would be the time for all nations to have true leaders to help bring about a new beginning. He would be the one for America—for the world.

But now was the time when he would have to make carefully thought out decisions on how to handle the situation in Iraq while the rest of the world was screaming for bloody vengeance. He could not afford to lose perspective and let his judgment be swayed by the popular vote. He had to be strong willed and determined to see through to the truth.

Kimball did have the support of the one person who was most important to him—his loving wife, Penny. She was the rock he held onto when he needed reassurance.

In a private sitting room adjoining a

conference room, Kimball was preparing to reveal his decision on whether or not to call for an air strike on Iraq in retaliation for the U.N. ambush. A decision no clear thinking man made easily. As he stood in front of a wall mirror, adjusting his tie, his wife Penny stood behind him. The future first couple reflected in the mirror. She was a pretty woman in her mid-forties with a smart, First Lady look about her. A combination of Jackie Kennedy's beauty and Eleanor Roosevelt's sophistication.

"Here, let me help you," she said in a soft, supporting voice. "I know that things don't always go our way. President Robbin's terrible accident has thrust you into office before your time and at a crucial moment in history." She finished with his tie and picked up his suit jacket from a chair in front of a small writing desk and helped him on with it. "But I just want to say that I am so proud of the way you've handled everything and I know that you're going to do the right thing."

Kimball turned around and faced his wife, putting his arms around her waist, holding her close. "That means the world to me. You give me the ability to remain strong in these difficult times--difficult decisions. I think the course of action we're about to take is best for the country and the rest of the world."

Kimball kissed his wife before letting her go, then stepped back to ask her approval. "How do I look?"

"Presidential."

"I love you."

"I love you too. Now go get them, tiger."

The conference room was alive with the sounds of a cacophony of voices from a room full of people talking all at once. They belonged to the four heads of the military, the Secretary of Defense, and several presidential advisors all sitting down at a long conference table. A quick silence came over the room as Kimball walked in. He shut the door behind him with one last quick wink back at Penny, then stood there for a moment, getting a feel of the room.

"Gentlemen, there have been some rather interesting developments with the situation in Iraq. Not more than one hour ago, I spoke on the phone with U.N. Secretary Mohammed Rahman, who informs me that Saddam is ready to allow the inspections of restricted sites."

Everyone remained silent as Kimball walked to the end of the conference room table. They all looked like this wasn't something they were expecting to hear.

Kimball took a seat at the end of the table, continuing his unexpected announcement. "This decision by Saddam to cooperate with the U.N. Special Council comes after many long negotiations with Secretary Rahman, and Saddam's insistence that he is being set up as a patsy. Saddam still proclaims his country's innocence in any involvement with the U.N. inspection team ambush, and Secretary Rahman informs me that he believes Saddam."

This small revelation caused quite a stir of garbled conversations among the men seated at the table.

"You can't trust Saddam. Rahman's a fool for believing him!" Marine General Robertson exclaimed.

"This is just a trick to call back our forces in the Gulf," Admiral Brown concluded.

"If Saddam didn't do it, then who did?" a young Harvard grad from the mid-west who was the youngest presidential advisor ever appointed asked.

This last statement caused Kimball to stand up, pushing his chair back across the floor. Everyone shut up and all eyes were on Kimball.

"That's exactly what we have to explore. Because if Saddam didn't do it, that means that there is someone out there manipulating the situation and I will not stand for that."

CHAPTER TWENTY TWO

The morning sunshine brightened Halprin's hotel room as the day began. Halprin and Kate were sleeping in bed. He was laying on his back and she was curled up along his side--nuzzled in tight and cozy, just beginning to stir awake.

While moving to sit up, Kate passed her hand over Halprin's chest, unexpectedly causing him to abruptly wake up. He sat up in bed in one quick motion, forcing Kate to move over. She was taken by surprise by Halprin's sudden movement.

"Jack! I hope that's not how you wake up every morning."

Halprin was still getting his bearings as he found his composure. "No. Not really."

Kate looked like she didn't believe him, but the phone rang and saved him from further explanation. He reached over and picked up the receiver after its second ring. "Hello." He paused for a second, recognizing the voice. "What's up Sam?"

As he listened, the unheard conversation he was privy to caused him to find the floor with his feet, sitting up on the side of the bed, opposite Kate.

"I'll be right down," he said, then hung up the phone and started getting dressed. As he got to his feet while pulling up his pants, he turned to face Kate. "There's been another murder."

"Who, Jack?" Kate got out of bed and also began getting dressed.

"One of the island girls who was with one of my men. They think he did it."

"Oh, god no."

****

Parker along with the rest of the men from Halprin's unit, excluding Walker, had gathered in the hotel bar. Parker sat at the bar with Stella behind it, pouring him a cup of coffee. The others were all hanging out patiently nearby.

Halprin walked into the bar by himself and right over to Parker. Kate stayed in the lobby to call Joan and have her meet them at the Paradise Nightclub. They would need all the help they could get with the local authorities.

"I'm going over to the crime scene," Halprin told Parker as he walked over. "I want you and the men to stay put and be ready."

Parker got off his barstool to talk to Halprin face to face. "Don't go getting yourself all worked up. You don't even know any of the facts other than the girl Sgt. Hunt was associated with was murdered."

"Sam, trust me on this. There's something big going down and this island is a part of it."

"All right, Jack. Go check things out. We'll hold down the fort," Parker said knowing that once Jack got his mind set on something, nothing could stop him.

"Just be ready for anything," Halprin warned before leaving.

"What's going on, Sam?" Stella asked from behind the bar.

"I'm not sure anymore. There are to many bodies turning up."

****

Several official vehicles were parked in front of the cottages of the Paradise Nightclub when Halprin and Kate pulled up in Halprin's rent-a-car. He parked next to Joan's army jeep, which was next to

Constable Moulin's official car, the coroner's wagon, and two island police cars.

"Think there were any witnesses?" Kate asked as they approached the first cottage, which was the center of attention.

"Only deaf, dumb and blind ones," Halprin answered skeptically as they walked up the front of the steps of the first cottage.

Halprin and Kate entered the cottage and came upon the sight of Mara tied to the bed with her throat slit open and her blood spread over her chest and the bed. Kate turned her head.

"Maybe you should wait outside," Halprin suggested putting a comforting hand on her shoulder.

"That won't be necessary, I'm fine," Kate insisted, quickly composing herself, trying to look as military as possible.

A police photographer snapped a couple of pictures of Mara, then stepped aside. As he moved out the way, Joan could be seen arguing with Constable Moulin.

"You don't have any proof that Sgt. Hunt did this, Moulin," Joan protested.

"That's Constable Moulin, Major Harris, and I have plenty of proof with these blood-soaked dog tags." Moulin held out Walker's dog tags, after picking them up off the floor with his pen. "Naming my suspect, a known associate of the victim. Plus if Sgt. Hunt didn't do this then where is he? Why does he not turn himself in?"

"Because he is probably dead."

Both Joan and Constable Moulin were surprised by Halprin's conclusion as they became aware of his and Kate's presence and turned to look at them.

"Who are you and what makes you believe that?"

"Captain Halprin. I'm Sgt. Hunter's CO and I know there is no way he did this," Halprin stated as he and Kate walked into the room. "He was in love with this girl and since it has been proven he was here, I must conclude that whoever did this was after him."

"It sounds to me like you're protecting your man, Captain. This was obviously a sex game that got out of control," Moulin said rejecting Halprin's theory as he pointed at Mara. "She's tied to the bed, there are numerous signs of forced sexual penetration. You would see it that way too, if you weren't connected."

Halprin was pissed off by Moulin's accusations. If I break his neck it might bring Walker back, Halprin thought.

"Why don't we step outside and get some air?" Joan suggested sensing Halprin's anger toward Moulin. "I'm sure that we will eventually find out what happened here."

Everyone agreed with Joan's idea, but that was about it. Both Moulin and Halprin had developed an instant dislike for each other.

They all exited the cottage and Moulin gave the okay to the coroner to remove the body as he lit a cigarette.

"Let me assure you, Captain that I will find out what happened and if you or any of your men interfere with this investigation I will charge you as accessories after the fact. Is that clear?" Moulin sneeringly informed him.

Halprin wanted to reach out and grab Moulin by his wimpy throat, but Kate was there to put a hand on his shoulder as she spoke for him.

"I know that Captain Halprin will assist you in your investigation in any way he and his men can," Kate assured Moulin.

"Yeah. Anything you need," Halprin reluctantly agreed with Kate's diplomatic approach, realizing it would be the best for now.

Further diffusing the situation, Moulin got a call on his cellular phone, which rang in his pocket. He answered it and walked a few feet away.

"Yes, I understand. I'll be there in twenty minutes," Moulin said. He put the phone back in his pocket and walked back over to the others. "I have other affairs to attend to, but I will be wanting to talk with and your men later on today, Captain Halprin. Please make yourself and your men available."

"No problem," Halprin said remaining cooperative. "We'll be at the hotel and maybe by then I'll have proof of my man's innocence."

Moulin sniffed the air at Halprin as he walked away and got in his car.

No one was sorry to see him go as he drove away. Joan, Halprin, and Kate huddled in conversation over their next move.

"Do you have any idea what happened or where your man is, Captain?" Joan asked frankly.

"It's a set up!" Halprin was positive in his response. "Walker was keeping an eye on the mercenaries for me and I think I got him killed."

"You mustn't think like that, Jack," Kate disagreed with Halprin's self-imposed blame.

"Why the set up? Why go through the trouble?" Joan wondered.

"It's a diversion. But from what?" Halprin answered cryptically.

CHAPTER TWENTY-THREE

Four black Humvees and Yusov's Land Rover were parked in front of the Governor's Mansion, along with Hubert's BMW. Forty mercenaries were waiting around smoking cigarettes, prepared for battle. An elite band of tough guys, clad in black fatigues and armed with automatic weapons—AK-47 Russian assault rifles being the weapon of choice.

Moulin pulled up in his official car and had to park out near the front gate, due to the full driveway. He got out and lit a cigarette while walking up to the house. Unfazed by the presence of the mercenaries standing around, he walked up to the front entrance and right in without knocking.

There was no reason why Moulin should be impressed by the mercenary army. He was well aware of Yusov's plan and had been in on it since its conception. Truth be known, it was initially his idea that got the ball rolling. He had spent most of his life on the islands and knew them well. He befriended Hubert and lured him into his confidence as he rose to power. But Moulin had an itch he couldn't scratch. He wanted to be the man in charge, wear the white suit, live in the big mansion. Yusov was his ticket. Yusov promised him all that and more.

Moulin first met Yusov through Santiago, ten years ago, when they both had a steady business arrangement. Yusov had developed a keen interest in the islands over the years since the end of the cold war and the fall of the former Soviet Union, knowing that one day he could use them to his advantage. And now that day had finally come.

As he walked down the entrance hall, Moulin could hear Hubert's raised, irate voice carrying out into the hallway entrance from the dining room.

"This is not what I agreed to, Yusov. You misrepresented your intentions here and I cannot allow you to proceed in this manner."

Moulin knew the source of Hubert's distress and also that he was in for a few more surprises. He walked into the room and stood near the doorway, surveying the room as he looked over at Yusov, who was wearing an expensive suit, looking more like a businessman than a mercenary. Nine of Yusov's men also wore business suits, including Demetri. They were standing around the long dining table, except for Yusov, who was sitting at the head of the table. Demetri stood by his side, holding the gray suitcase from Santiago's yacht in his hand. One of Yusov's men, Vadmir, an effeminate man with oval glasses, long side burns, and a thin mustache, was also sitting at the table. He was working on a portable computer and filled one of the most integral parts of Yusov's plan. He was a computer expert who was hacking into the S.M.A.R.T. Station's computer to implant a virus that would shut down the satellite link and blind the world to what they were really up to.

Hubert let out a sigh of relief as he noticed Moulin, who remained stoic. "Now, I'm going to put a stop to this," Hubert announced while walking over to Moulin, but Yusov's voice stopped him from behind with his familiarity toward Moulin.

"It is good to see you again, Jacques. I hope everything is in order."

Hubert stood in the middle of the room and slowly turned back to Yusov .

"You two know each other?"

"Like I said, Governor," a smiling Yusov responded. "I'm always ready to plan around any contingencies. Especially the ones I can clearly see. I knew there would be no problem securing a camp, or even getting you to bring me along with you to the embassy dinner tonight as an invited guest. You like having your finger on the pulse of both legal and illegal political activities, while staying neutral. But I also knew that once you got to close to the fire you would back away like a butterfly with scorched wings. That is where Jacques comes in, Governor, cause you see there is no turning back this time. You're going to fly straight into the sun and it's going to be a hell of a ride."

Hubert looked back, disappointingly, at Moulin who remained expressionless, then back at Yusov. He slumped his shoulders knowing he had no choice but to go along with Yusov's plan. Moulin controlled the island police force and some of the guns in the Seychelles, while Yusov controlled the rest. Checkmate. He had really gotten in over his head. There was nothing he could do. "Like I said, a man of great resolve."

"You have no idea," Yusov responded triumphantly.

Vadmir looked up from his portable computer with a satisfied expression of accomplishment. "It is done, comrade Yusov. The virus is ready to be implanted in the tracking station mainframe."

"Very good, comrade Vadmir," Yusov commended as he stood up along with Vadmir. "It is time."

Demetri led the other mercenaries out of the room, while Yusov walked over to Hubert and put his arm around his shoulder like an old buddy as he walked him out. "Don't look so worried, Governor. Soon it will all be over and if you do as you're told, you'll be a very rich man."

Yusov stopped at the doorway, by Moulin. "Now, go wait outside. I'll be along in a moment."

Hubert gave Moulin another stunned look. "You are a real disappointment to me, Jacques. How could you do this to me after all I've done for you?"

"You did it to yourself, Marcel."

Hubert left the room and headed outside, a defeated man.

Yusov led Moulin down the entrance hall as Moulin lit another cigarette. He offered Yusov one, but he turned it down. Moulin nervously puffed on his cigarette. He knew his part in Yusov's mission had become even more important with the surprise presence of the U.S. Special Forces unit on the island. He was just supposed to keep things in order when Yusov took over the S.M.A.R.T. Station and knew handling Hubert wouldn't be a problem. But this Captain Halprin was not someone easily fooled or manipulated. Or someone who would give up or just go away.

Yusov sensed Moulin's apprehension as he probed for information. "What do you have for me?'"

"This Captain Halprin from that Special Forces unit is a tough case, and might be a problem if left alone. I'm sure it was him who told his man to watch you. He also knows that his man is being framed. He's real suspicious, but doesn't know anything substantial. He's just fishing around."

"Do you know where they are?"

"He said they would be at the Hilton."

Yusov stopped at the open front door, as did Moulin. He didn't appear to be concerned about Halprin and his men and was casual in his demeanor about how to deal with them. "Round them up, tell them you need statements,   then take them somewhere and kill them all."

"What if they won't go?" Moulin asked nervously, not expressing any morality about cold-blooded murder, but rather more a concern of accomplishing it.

"Kill them where they stand, if you have to," Yusov said callously as he walked outside.

Klaus was waiting on the front steps, wearing a local police uniform. He came to attention, along with all the men waiting near the Humvees, as Yusov stepped outside.

Moulin stepped out and noticed Klaus wearing the local police uniform.

"Comrade Yusov, everything is set and we await your command," Klaus announced while still standing at attention.

"Very good comrade. Today we shall become a part of history."

"You seem to have thought of everything," Moulin added.

"Nothing can be left to chance," Yusov said addressing his subordinates. He headed over toward Hubert's BMW with Moulin and Klaus following. "You shall take care of business in town with Klaus, and shut down all outgoing communication at their source."

Yusov stopped by Hubert and the BMW with his Land Rover parked behind it. The others wearing suits were also waiting there. Demetri was still holding the gray suitcase.

"And the good Governor, here, is going to earn his money by escorting us to the embassy dinner."

"Whatever you say, Andrei. You are calling the shots now," Hubert said with an understanding that he had no choice except to do as he was told if he wanted to see the morning again.

"Don't look so sad, Governor. Your precious island will still be here after we're gone and no one will care about what happens here today. Tomorrow, there will be more imperative matters to attend to."

CHAPTER TWENTY-FOUR

Both Joan's jeep and Halprin's rent-a-car were parked in front of the entrance gate to the mercenary camp. Kate, Joan, and Halprin stood outside the gate, looking over the empty camp grounds.

"We're two late," Halprin stated.

"Where did they all go?" Kate asked.

"I don't know and I don't like it," Joan admitted.

"Whatever they're up to is going down soon. I think we should get back to the hotel and check if any of my men have seen anything," Halprin suggested.

"Maybe Sgt. Hunt showed up," Kate said hopefully.

"Maybe," Halprin said with little conviction.

"You two go on ahead, I'm going to stop by Hubert's place and have a talk with him and find out who these mercenaries are, then I'll meet you back at the hotel," Joan said.

"Good idea," Halprin agreed.

CHAPTER TWENTY-FIVE

The sun was sinking on the horizon with the Governor's BMW leading the way to the S.M.A.R.T. Station and Yusov's Land Rover following behind. The mood inside the BMW was rather somber for Hubert. He knew everything he had worked so hard for was about to come to a bad end, all because he allowed this madman access to his island. He should have been more suspicious when Yusov insisted on joining him at the annual embassy dinner which was given each year to build better public relations with all the foreign dignitaries that were stationed there. Hubert just thought that Yusov wanted an audience to voice his credo. The most trouble he ever thought would come from the evening would be a heated argument over the evils of democracy and the capitalistic demons who control the world. This was the kind of political tripe that he had been subject to since Yusov arrived. Hubert personally couldn't care less about politics unless it helped his position. But as they approached the front entrance gate to the embassy and S.M.A.R.T. Station, Hubert knew exactly what Yusov really wanted.

The guard at the front gate came to attention and the one inside the guard booth came out with a clipboard as the BMW pulled up first with Land Rover behind. The back passenger side window of the BMW slid down on its motorized track as the guard with the clipboard stopped by the car, bent over, and peered inside.

Hubert was sitting next to the open window with Yusov at his side. The guard appeared in the window as he addressed Hubert with a welcome, expected familiarity.

"Go right on in, Governor Hubert. Ambassador Neville is expecting you and your dinner guests." He waved them through without any concern.

"Thank you. Sergeant," Hubert said smiling nervously back at the guard.

The Governor's BMW pulled through the entrance gate followed by the Land Rover, driven by Demetri. Both vehicles parked in the visitor's lot. The Governor's driver got out and opened the door for Hubert. Yusov followed Hubert out of the car. They were accompanied by two beautiful female mercenaries, Sonja and Nikki, who were dressed in evening gowns.

Yusov looked over at Demetri getting out of the Land Rover, giving him a silent signal with his eyes. Demetri did the same thing to two of the mercenaries, Franco and Darius, from the Land Rover. While Demetri and the other mercenaries joined Yusov and

Hubert, Franco and Darius lagged behind. They both pulled out 9mm automatic handguns and attached silencers while keeping their backs turned away from the entrance gate.

Demetri was carrying the gray suitcase from Santiago's yacht and Vadmir had his computer case in hand as they all headed for the front entrance. Yusov and Hubert led the way with Nikki and Sonja on their arms. The other five mercenaries brought up the rear and appeared to be concealing weapons under their suit jackets.

As the others entered the tracking station/embassy lobby, Franco and Darius headed over toward the front gate. They got within ten feet of the two marines, who were unaware of their approach until it was too late. The guard with the clipboard was walking back to his booth when he saw the two armed men coming at them. He only had time to raise his hand and open his mouth, but no words came out. Franco shot him twice in the chest. As the other guard came rushing around the gate, alerted by the sound of the body falling to the ground, he was shot dead by Darius.

****

Ambassador Neville came walking up from the embassy hallway to greet his dinner guests. He appeared to be in a jovial mood putting forth his most diplomatic face in hopes of easing the tension that had been building since the Treasure Seeker tragedy.

Neville maintained his chipper attitude as he reached Hubert and his guests, but there was something wrong with the way Hubert looked at him. He looked like a bad child who was caught doing something wrong.

"Harold, I'm sorry for this. It is not want I wanted," Hubert said offering Neville his hand with his head down, unable to look him in the eyes.

Neville just looked confused as he shook Hubert's hand, but his confusion was soon cleared up as Yusov pulled out his piece.

"What is going on here, Marcel?" Neville asked, his good mood quickly disappearing.

Sonja and Nikki also pulled out automatic handguns from discretely concealed hiding places under their dresses. Then they both moved in closer to Neville, taking him by the arms, rubbing their pistol barrels up along his chest in an alluring, seductive style.

"I thought that it would be obvious, Ambassador Neville," Yusov said calmly. "I'm taking over the island and this S.M.A.R.T. Station, and as long as you do as you're told, I'll let you all live."

Neville was speechless. Meanwhile, Franco and Darius made their way into the station, brandishing their weapons, leading the other mercenaries, who had removed weapons from their suit jackets.

Yusov extended his arm down the hallway pointing to the S.M.A.R.T. Room, wanting Neville to lead the way. "Ambassador, would you mind. I believe your presence will help subdue any resistance."

"You'll never get away with this," Neville retorted, pissing his pants.

"I already have."

Neville started off down the hallway with Nikki and Sonja at his side. Yusov escorted Hubert while Demetri and Vadmir followed. The muffled sounds of Franco's and Darius' silencer equipped handguns were heard just before Neville and company entered the S.M.A.R.T. Room.

As he entered the room, Neville came upon the sight of two dead marines and all of the communications specialists with their hands raised above their heads. Franco and Darius stood near the doorway still holding their guns in the direction of the dead marines, while five other mercenaries pointed weapons at the commo specialists.

Yusov guided Hubert into the room as Demetri and Vadmir entered behind them. Demetri handed the gray suitcase to Yusov as Vadmir went over to the communications console with his computer case.

Colonel Vanderweel walked in from the other end of the room, down by the officer's offices. "What's all this commotion about?" he asked harshly.

Before Vanderweel could get an answer, he was quickly targeted in by Darius and Franco.

"Just borrowing your facility for an old magician's trick. It will be an illusion the whole world will be witness to, but never know it," Yusov boasted proudly to Vanderweel.

CHAPTER TWENTY-SIX

The sunset was almost over and darkness began to set in when Halprin and Kate arrived at the hotel—before Joan. They pulled up front in Halprin's rent-a-car and parked on the street. The hotel was located on a hill with the main road leading both down to the marina and up to the S.M.A.R.T. Station. As Halprin and Kate got out of the rent-a-car, which was facing up a hill, Halprin looked up the road and saw two black Humvees stopping next to the Communication Building, about two hundred yards up from the hotel.

Kate noticed that Halprin was focused on something up the road as she started to head for the lobby entrance.

"What is it, Jack?" she asked curiously, following his line of sight just as Constable Moulin's official car appeared over a rise in the road. It headed toward the hotel with another Humvee following it.

"I don't know, but I don't like it," Halprin said realizing that things were about to get hot. "Let's get inside."

Halprin and Kate headed for the bar entrance, instead of the lobby.

Parker was sitting at the bar smoking a cigar. Stella was behind the bar, but there were no other customers other than Parker, who immediately stood up as Halprin and Kate entered the bar, alerted by their abrupt entrance.

"What's going on, Jack?" Parker asked sensing Halprin's heightened state of readiness. "A constable Moulin called and said he was coming down to get statements.

He particularly wanted to know if you and the men were here."

Kate and Halprin looked at each other with the sudden realization that statements were not what Moulin was after.

"Sam, you got to listen to me," Halprin said with a strong sense of urgency. "Moulin is in the thick of what is going down on this island and it's happening as we speak. He's on his way here with mercenary back-up and believe me, they don't want statements.

Stella expressed her concern for their safety as she reached over from behind the bar and put a hand on Parker's shoulder. "You can't trust Moulin, Sam."

"I believe you both," Parker said as he looked over at Stella, then back at Halprin. "So what is the plan?"

"Where are the men?" Halprin asked, taking command.

"Upstairs," Parker answered affirmatively. "I told them to hang out and have dinner in their rooms. Stella's got a line behind the bar and can call them down."

"Do it."

As Stella picked up the phone behind the bar to call upstairs, Kate got an idea of her own.

"I will call the station and let them know that something is going on," Kate said as she moved behind the bar while Stella finished her call then handed her the receiver.

"I think they already know," Halprin said as he put it all together. He started to quickly assess their position while looking around the bar.

"I can't get an answer at the station or the embassy," Kate said slightly bewildered.

"I didn't think you would," Halprin said knowingly. Try Major Harris' jeep."

I should be able to get through to her. Kate thought as she dialed the number.

"What the hell do the want with the S.M.A.R.T. Station?" Parker wondered.

"They can't do anything from there, except monitor traffic."

"Maybe the bad guys figured out a way they could use it to hide something," Halprin theorized.

"Hide what?" Parker asked.

Before they could ponder this further, Kate got through to Joan's jeep.

"Joan, there's something strange going on. I can't get through to the station or the embassy," Kate said into the phone.

****

A little ways up the road, a squad of heavily armed mercenaries led by Garcia and Sergi stormed into the communication building, which handled all telephone, cellular, fax, and internet communication capabilities for the island. Everyone in the building was taken by total surprise with the sudden hostile takeover.

"Who is in charge, here?" Garcia demanded.

"I am," an old man in a cheap business suit said stepping forward.

Garcia pistol-whipped him across the face. "No you're not. I am. Now I want you to shut everything down. Or die!"

Sergi signaled the other mercenaries, who immediately surrounded the communication technicians and their equipment while pointing guns at them.

****

Moulin, Klaus, and four local law enforcement officers—who arrived in a police wagon to haul Halprin and his men away—had gathered outside the hotel lobby entrance. There was also a Humvee with a squad of mercenaries waiting just up the road a bit, in case of resistance.

Armed only with side arms, Moulin, Klaus, and the four locals walked in the hotel lobby entrance.

Kate was still on the hotel bar with Joan, but was caught off in mid-sentence. "I don't know what's going on, but I think you should get here as.....Joan. Hello. Joan." Kate held out the receiver as she looked over to Halprin. "It just went dead."

"They are isolating the island from the rest of the world," Halprin concluded.

"But why?" Parker wanted to know.

Halprin and Parker were standing in front of the bar near the hotel entrance. Kate was still standing behind the bar, along with Stella.

Moulin and Klaus walked into the bar from the hotel lobby, followed by their flunkies.

Moulin and Klaus stopped about five feet in front of Halprin and Parker, while the others waited by the doorway.

"Captain Halprin," Moulin started things off. "How fortunate to find you here. Sgt. Major Parker told me you were out when

I called, and I see you have Captain Allen with you, too."

Kate remained behind the bar with Stella.

Halprin was standing directly in front of Moulin, and Klaus in front of Parker.

Parker gave Klaus a familiar look of recognition, but was unable to place where from. Klaus looked back at Parker with the same look of recognition, only he knew it came from the same bar, two nights ago.

There was tension in the room—thick enough to cut with a machete.

"What can I do for you, Constable Moulin?" Halprin asked. "Would you like those statements now?"

"Yes, Captain Halprin. As a matter of fact, I wanted to get statements from you and all of your men at the same time," Moulin said in an easy manner. "I have a wagon outside to take you all to the police station in order to get this over as quickly as possible."

"I don't think so, Constable Moulin," Halprin objected. "If you want anything from me and my men then I suggest we do it here and now."

Parker was still trying to remember where he saw Klaus before, making Klaus apprehensive. Halprin's refusal to cooperate just made matters more tense.

Out in the hotel lobby stairway, which came down in between the bar entrance and the lobby entrance, the nine remaining men from Halprin's unit cautiously made their way down the stairs, being careful not to draw attention to themselves.

Reid, the second weapons expert, was in the lead. He was followed by Fuller, the demo man. Reid raised his hand for everyone to hold up as the now heightened conversation between Halprin and Moulin drifted into the lobby from the bar.

"What do you mean, Captain? I have prepared everything back at the police station for your arrival," Moulin's upset voice echoed out into the lobby.

"I don't care!" Halprin's raised voice carried a disgruntled tone. "You have no grounds to try and force me or my men to go anywhere with you."

At that point, Kate came around from behind the bar and walked over to Halprin's side. "You are overstepping your bounds of authority here, Constable."

"Stop stalling and lets get this over with," Klaus said angrily, getting impatient with Moulin's lack of force in his approach to dealing with Halprin.

"Please maintain your composure," Moulin protested to Klaus' whose hand was already moving down toward his side.

The four cops behind Moulin also sensed the potential confrontation and readied themselves for action.

Kate looked at Halprin and they appeared to both feel the precariousness of their position and that a confrontation was inevitable.

Parker ignited the final spark that set things into motion as he realized Klaus' true identity. "Hey, Jack. This guy is one of those mercenaries from the bar..."

Parker raised his arm and pointed his finger at Klaus, but was cut off as Klaus plunged his knife into Parker's stomach.

"Not here, you fool," Moulin yelled out as he and the four cops drew their guns and pointed them at the unarmed Kate and Halprin, ignoring Stella behind the bar.

Klaus didn't care about Moulin's objections as he extracted his knife from Parker. "I'm through fucking around here."

Parker turned and fell forward against the bar, propping himself up while looking toward his friend.

Halprin's eyes filled with enraged sadness as he reached out to Parker, knowing his friend was dying.

As Parker started to slip away, he turned to look at Stella, giving her a last wink before collapsing to the floor, dead.

Stella appeared to collapse with a shriek of grief behind the bar, but instead reappeared immediately with a twelve gauge shotgun. She then pumped two quick shots into the surprised Klaus, as he had time to watch his chest explode before falling dead to the floor in a bloody mess. "Take that you son-of-a-bitch," she cried out.

Moulin and the four cops reacted more out of instinct than awareness as they all concentrated their fire at Stella, shooting her several times.

Halprin pushed Kate to the floor as the bullets flew past them. It was time to rumble. Halprin's men charged into the room from the hallway, with Reid and Fuller in the lead. They easily overtook the four cops from behind, who were no match for them. Halprin's men showed no mercy as they dispatched the four cops with various hand to hand, bone crushing, assault tactics, breaking necks while stripping them of their guns in the process.

Moulin, the weasel that he was, managed to break through as he ran away while shooting wildly behind him, making it out of the bar entrance. Reid and Fuller went after him, while Fergusen and Kelly, the two medics, checked out Parker and Stella.

Moulin stumbled on the road outside of the bar in a fearful panic. He fell to the ground, scrapping his hand, then staggered to his feet as he ran for cover. "Get them! They killed everyone!" he shouted as he took cover behind the Humvee, which had moved to a closer position.

The ten mercenaries from the Humvee started to move in on the hotel, firing automatic weapons at the bar entrance. Reid and Fuller emerged from the bar for a few seconds before being forced back inside by a barrage of bullets.

Halprin was kneeling down beside his dead friend with Kate at his side as Reid and Fuller came running back in with bullets hot on their trail. Miller, the second demo specialist, and Cooper, a communication specialist, had the other two confiscated pistols and supplied cover for Reid and Fuller.

Halprin quickly got to his feet and yelled to Kelly who was behind the bar checking Stella. "Kelly! Throw me that shotgun."

Halprin had only to reach out his hand as the shotgun came flying up over the bar as if on command alone. Two mercenaries made it to the doorway of the bar as Reid and Fuller stood to the side of the heavy oak doors. They fired a hail of bullets into the room, which impacted all around Halprin, chipping wood from the bar, but missing him. Halprin on the other hand was true to his aim and blasted both mercenaries as they entered the room. Reid and Fuller then managed to get the doors closed.

Cooper and Miller, along with the others, barricaded the entrance with tables and chairs.

"We only have a couple of minutes before they regroup and come back at us with all they got," Halprin said taking command of the situation. "So, what is our weapons status, Sgt. Reid?"

Reid quickly took inventory of the supplies. "We have four nine millimeter automatics with one clip apiece, plus that shotgun, sir."

"Got one box of shells. Half empty," Kelly called out from behind the bar.

Fuller looked past Kelly and behind the bar at the liquor bottles. "Miller, give me a hand," he said while walking over to the bar. "We also have an unlimited supply of molotov cocktails."

While Fuller and Miller prepared the liquor bottles with ripped up bar rags for fuses, Halprin conferred with Kate on their next move.

"We got to figure a way out of here and up to the S.M.A.R.T. Station," Halprin said while looking around for another exit.

"Joan was on her way there when we got cut off. Maybe she was able to get through to the S.M.A.R.T. Station," Kate said optimistically. Still shaken by the gunfight and more dead bodies than she had ever dreamed of seeing in her life.

"I wouldn't count on it. Something tells me that the station and embassy have been taken over or else they would never have pulled this shit," Halprin concluded.

****

Moulin directed the mercenaries to concentrate their attack from the street as they lined up in front of the bar and opened fire. The eight mercenaries left took cover behind Halprin' rent-a-car and blasted away at the bar, the bullets shattering the long, narrow, dark tinted windows.

While cowering behind the Humvee, Moulin used a hand held radio to call for reinforcements from the mercenaries holding the communication building. "Unit Two and Three send back up. Command Leader One is down. We need help, now!"

Across the street from Moulin and down at the corner intersection in front of the Chez T'ed restaurant, Joan's jeep pulled up to the corner and stopped. From where she sat, Joan had a clear view of the mercenary assault on the hotel bar, with the sound of gun fire echoing out in the falling night. A street light gave off a silhouette impression of Joan. She had the jeep's radio phone in her hand, which she tossed to the floor in frustration. She reached over, opened the glove compartment, and removed a pistol. After removing the clip to make sure it was loaded, she slammed it back home. "Time to kick butt," she said as she gritted her teeth and punched the gas.

****

The mercenaries' bullets were blasting in all around the bar room while Kate, Halprin, and his men took cover behind the bar. Halprin had the shotgun gripped tightly in his hands, with bullets flying over his head. Kate was crouched down beside him with Reid next to her. They each had a confiscated pistol. Fuller and Miller were next to Reid and they all had liquor bottles in their hands with rag fuses. Behind them were Stark and Roth, the intelligence specialists, and they also held onto liquor bottles with rag fuses, and behind them, Fergusen and Kelly with the other confiscated pistols. The rear was held up by the communication specialists, Cooper and Jones, who were also armed with liquor bottle bombs.

The hail of bullets was causing severe damage to the bar room as wood chips flew and lamp fixtures fell as the structure weakened.

"We better get out of here before this place comes down on our heads," Kate said as the urgency of their situation started to settle in.

"When they stop to reload, we'll make our move for the door and try to get to the car," Halprin commanded. Knowing that not all of the bad guys would reload at the same time. Hell, it was a good time to die.

"We won't all be able to fit," Kate feared.

"We'll make it fit," Halprin said firmly.

****

Joan rolled down her window as she headed straight toward the mercenaries positioned behind Halprin's rent-a-car. As she closed in on them, she extended her arm out the window, with her pistol in hand, and fired at the unsuspecting mercenaries, who, in the heat of action, were unaware of her approach.

Moulin was still on the radio when his attention was drawn to the sound of Joan's shooting. He looked over just in time to see Joan take out two of the eight mercenaries. She didn't slow down as she closed in on the bar, but instead managed to take out another mercenary before ramming her jeep right through the bar wall.

The jeep easily broke through the wall and came all the way into the bar before stopping.

"Somebody call for a taxi?" Joan quipped.

Kate, Halprin, and his men got to their feet, taking their cue that it was time to leave.

"You sure know how to make an entrance," Kate said happy to see Joan.

"Come on, men, lets take it to them," Halprin yelled out as he led the charge out of the new exit Joan had created.

Kate got into the jeep and Joan threw it into reverse and backed out the way she came as Halprin and his men took it to the street.

Halprin exited shooting the shotgun, blasting away two mercenaries. Reid took out two more as Fuller and Miller threw the lit liquor bombs on the street, creating a firewall between Halprin's rent-a-car and the mercenaries' Humvee. The others did the same with their liquor bombs, with one bottle hitting the last mercenary, which engulfed him in flames. Reid shot him dead—a burning man can still fire a gun.

Halprin got into the driver's seat of his car while his men divided up between Joan's jeep and the rent-a-car, after policing up the dead mercenaries discarded weapons.

Moulin watched through the flames as his mission went awry. He was not defeated, though, as one of the Humvees from the communication building made it down the road, followed by two police cars.

"Seal off the road to the station," Moulin barked out orders into the radio. "Don't let them past at any cost."

Back on the other side of the flames, both Halprin and Joan saw the reinforcements coming and realized they were outgunned. Their vehicles were side by side after Halprin turned his car around, now facing down the road toward the marina.

"They've blocked off the road to the station. We're not going to be able to get through. We don't have enough fire power," Joan yelled over to Halprin.

Halprin could see Santiago's yacht standing out in the marina, only a quarter mile away. "Follow me. I know where we can get some," Halprin said, peeling out down the road.

Joan followed, leaving Moulin and the mercenaries behind.

CHAPTER TWENTY-SEVEN

Yusov was in the S.M.A.R.T. Room, listening to his radiophone and from his angry expression it was easy to ascertain that he didn't like what he heard.

"What do you mean they got past you," Yusov yelled into the phone. "I don't care if they can't get up here. I want them dead. You see to it Moulin or I'll come down there and feed you your balls.."

Yusov angrily shut off the radiophone and chucked it at Demetri, standing next to him. "They took out Klaus."

"That can't be," Demetri interjected. "How could they take out someone like Klaus?"

"Either they were very lucky or they're very good," Yusov said walking over to where Nikki and Sonja stood over Ambassador Neville and Colonel Vanderweel. They were the only ones left in the S.M.A.R.T. Room aside from Vadmir and Hubert. All the S.M.A.R.T. Room technicians and embassy personnel were being held in the cafeteria by Darius, Franco, and the other mercenaries.

Hubert was standing off to the side of Neville and Vanderweel, looking like a shameful outcast.

Yusov stopped in front of Vanderweel. "It seems like those Special Forces boys were able to temporarily get away from my men with the help of your Major Harris," Yusov said smiling snidely, amused by Joan's gender. "A female Marine Major. Must be a tough bitch. Isn't she, Colonel?"

Vanderweel ignored Yusov's inquires and offered his own opinion on Yusov's chances. "Do you really think you can start a war with a simple trick of misdirection?

There are too may other fail safe systems for the early detection of such attacks."

"By that time it will be too late," Yusov said grinning. "However, I do think it would be wise to pull out the file on your Major Harris."

Yusov moved over to where Vadmir was sitting down at one of the computer consoles, implanting the virus that would shut down the satellite tacking systems in the area.

"Comrade Vadmir, how long until you are ready?" Yusov asked.

"It will take about three hours to run its cycle, leaving plenty of time to spare before the morning launch," Vadmir said, looking up from the computer screen, which he had hooked into the S.M.A.R.T. mainframe computer.

"Very good comrade. See if you can punch up the military records of this Major Harris and Captain Halprin. I want to see exactly what we're dealing with."

CHAPTER TWENTY-EIGHT

The earlier commotion from the hotel didn't have any effect on the marina's peaceful existence. Over an hour had passed since the shoot out, and everyone was up by the hotel like moths drawn to a fire, leaving the boardwalk barren and empty.

There was a boat shed at the end of the marina, a decrepit tin frame building. The large sliding front door was opened a crack, revealing the moving shadows of its hidden occupants.

Both Joan's jeep and Halprin's rent-a-car were concealed in the boat shed, which didn't have any boats stored in it. Everyone gathered around, preparing for their next move and checking the ammo supply of their confiscated weapons.

"I sure hope you're right about this, Captain Halprin," Joan said as she slammed a fresh clip in her automatic, chambering the first round, then putting the safety on before sticking it in the back of her pants.

"I don't see that we have many options," Halprin said, loading the last few shells into the pump shotgun. "Fernando Santiago is involved in all of this somehow. Sgt. Hunt saw those mercenaries go aboard his yacht and he disappeared later that night. I know there's a connection and some of the answers we're looking for we'll find there."

Reid had a confiscated AK-47 from one of the dead mercenaries back at the hotel as did Fuller and Miller. The others only had handguns.

"Ready to deploy the men whenever you are, Captain," Reid informed Halprin as he took over the second in command position now that Parker and Walker were gone. "We are light on supplies, but we got enough guts for an entire army of mercenaries and arms dealers, sir."

"That is good to hear, Sgt. Reid. I think we're going to need them today. Take your positions."

Reid led Miller and Fuller over to the large sliding shed door, where Fergusen and Kelly waited. They slid back the large door on its creaky rollers without drawing too much attention.

"I wish we had more time to think up a better plan," Halprin said to Kate and Joan. Feeling responsible for having these two women risk their lives. They needed the element of surprise for the plan to work. Expect the unexpected.

"We'll be all right," Kate assured him.

"Lets do it then," Joan said firmly.

****

The cover of night helped to conceal Reid, Fuller, and Miller as they crept up along the boardwalk to Santiago's yacht, taking cover in the shadows. They each had an AK-47 and took tactical positions around the boardwalk stands to get a clear target of the yacht. They sighted in three armed guards patrolling around on the bow.

Kate and Joan walked right up the boardwalk in plain sight as she headed straight for Santiago's yacht.

Halprin and the rest of his men hung back by the boat shed, which was fifty yards from the yacht. They waited for Kate and Joan to reach the dockway leading to the yacht before moving down the boardwalk. Halprin had the shotgun under an old coat he found in the boat shed.

Two more armed guards were stationed at the bottom of the docking plank to the yacht and were alerted to Joan's and Kate's presence as they walked toward them.

"State your business here," the guard demanded while holding his rifle out in front of him to show he meant business.

"I'm Major Harris, from the embassy. I wanted to ask Fernando Santiago a few questions about the disappearance of a vacationing soldier."

The guard didn't know how to respond to this, but didn't have to think about it too long as Santiago appeared at the top of the boarding plank.

"You have no authority here," Santiago declared.

"I am aware of that," Joan agreed amiably. "I just thought that we might be able to help each other...on good faith."

"Now, how can you help me?" Santiago wanted to know.

As Halprin and his men reached the dockway, he gave the signal for the attack by blowing the guard away with his shotgun.

Joan pulled out her automatic from behind her back and coldly put a shot into the other guard's chest at point blank range. Then, three more shots rang out loudly in the quiet night as Reid, Fuller, and Miller took out the three guards on the bow with precision accuracy.

We can let you live," Joan said as she took aim at a stunned Santiago.

Halprin and the others charged up the docking plank while Joan kept Santiago covered. After Reid, Fuller, and Miller joined Halprin and the others on the yacht, Kate and Joan headed up the plank, with Joan keeping Santiago in gunsight.

On the yacht, Reid directed Fuller and Miller to take over the guards positions on the bow and watch for unwanted company. Fergusen and Kelly stayed by the top of the docking plank, after discarding the dead guards' bodies.

"Why have you murdered my men?" Santiago demanded.

Joan pushed Santiago toward the stateroom. Giving him a hard shove that spun him around. He stumbled inside while Joan kept him covered.

"We are commandeering this vessel and I'm charging you as a co-conspirator in the plot to takeover the embassy and S.M.A.R.T. Station. Which means, I can shoot you right where you stand."

"I'd do what the lady said if I were you," Halprin said impressed with Joan's toughness.

Halprin and Kate followed Joan into the stateroom.

"Reid take Stark and Roth on a search of the lower decks and see if you can find any weapons or anybody else hiding on the boat." Cooper, Jones. See if you can raise anybody on the radio. Try the embassy, first, and if you can't get through try the Seventh Fleet."

Cooper and Jones made their way over to the steering controls and the communication console, which was all controlled from the stateroom.

Joan had her gun barrel jammed against Santiago's throat as she forced him down on the Captain's chair. "I want to know what the hell is going on or so help me, I'll send you to a cold, dark place from where you'll never return. And don't even think about trying to bullshit me," she said as she rammed the pistol hard enough to make him gag.

Santiago was starting to sweat. "If you kill me, you'll never know. But how do I know you won't kill me if I tell you?"

"We don't have time for this," Joan said as she cocked her gun to show Santiago she meant business. "Because I'll kill you if you don't."

Halprin stepped over to Santiago, thinking that Joan just might shoot him. Kate was over by Cooper and Jones, who were unsuccessfully trying to raise anyone, when Fuller called in from out on the bow.

"Captain! We got company coming in fast," Fuller's voice carried into the stateroom.

Halprin, still clutching his shotgun, started out for the bow while yelling down to Reid and the others below. "Reid, get up here. We've got to move."

"It would seem that there's going to be enough killing to go around," Santiago mused.

"You'll die first," Joan assured him.

Halprin hurried past Joan and Santiago and out onto the bow to get a better view of the incoming traffic. As he reached Fuller and Miller, Moulin and the mercenaries drove up to the boardwalk. They all piled out of their vehicles and started blasting away at the yacht.

Halprin and his men took cover and returned fire, but soon ran out of ammo. But then, Reid, Stark and Roth came running up from the stateroom, providing cover with newly acquired weapons found in a secret cache on the lower decks.

Halprin looked up at Reid in approval. "Where did you find these?" he asked, referring to the weapons.

Reid answered him while continuing the attack. "We hit the jackpot, Captain." He had to yell over the sound of gunfire. "Santiago's got enough weapons for a hundred guys hidden on this boat."

Even with the added firepower, the incoming bullets were zinging around everywhere, getting intensely overpowering.

"I don't think we can hold up here much longer," Halprin stated as Reid handed him a rifle.

Then as if someone was reading Halprin's mind inside the yacht, the mighty boat's engines roared to life. Halprin looked in the cabin window and saw Kate at the controls. He nodded to her in silent approval. Retreat and fight another time and place.

Halprin directed Reid and the others to shoot away the docking ropes as the big boat started to move.

"Looks like we are going for a ride," Joan told Santiago.

"You are going to pay for this," Santiago threatened.

Halprin came back into the stateroom, while the others remained out on the bow, holding off the mercenaries. He headed over to the controls towards Kate, after seeing that Joan had Santiago well covered.

"How we doing? Can you handle this baby?" Halprin asked Kate.

"No problem," she answered. "Any ideas on where we should go?"

"Yeah," Halprin said positively. "Head out toward where the Treasure Seeker was last reported."

Kate looked at Halprin in understanding. That was where it all began.

As the yacht backed out of the marina and out into the wide open ocean, Moulin and the mercenaries continued their attack, but were unable to prevent the loss of their antagonists for a second time.

****

After driving out on the open water for a while, Kate brought the yacht to a stop. It just floated on the calm ocean water with a bright full moon hanging over the horizon.

Halprin and Joan were interrogating a screaming Santiago while Kate assisted Cooper and Jones, trying to raise somebody on the radio. The others were down in the lower decks getting supplies from Santiago's fully stocked armory hidden in the belly of the boat. Fergusen and Kelly were outside on watch in the dark night.

Santiago was still sitting down on the captain's chair, untied and indignant. "You can kill me if you want, but you won't stop anything."

"You better come clean or life expectancy will be the least of your problems," Halprin assured Santiago.

"You'll never find anything," Santiago said defiantly.

"Find what?" Joan asked instinctively.

Before Santiago could answer, Fergusen called in from the bow. "Captain! I think you better come and take a look at this."

As Halprin ran out on the bow, Fergusen was holding a search light and scanning the water. He focused the light on the rocky base of a barren island, shining on what appeared to be someone sprawled out on the rocks.

Halprin made it out to the end of the bow as it became clear that it was what was left of Walker laid out on the rocks. "Come on. Let's get him," Halprin said with enthusiasm in his voice to suggest that he thought he might still be alive.

Fergusen and Kelly proceeded back to the stern where the speedboat dingy was set up.

Back in the stateroom, Kate, Cooper, and Jones were distracted by the activities outside the yacht that Reid and the others were unaware of yet—being still in the lower decks.

Joan was keeping Santiago covered and turned her back for a moment to inquire about the communication hold up. "What's the progress on that radio, Kate?"

Santiago took this opportunity to make his move as Kate informed Joan that they were picking up something. "I think we might have raised the Nimitz," Kate answered as Santiago leapt from his chair and lunged at Joan.

Joan was unprepared for the attack and Santiago managed to gain the initiative as he tried to wrestle the gun from her hand. Santiago got control of the gun and fired two wild shots that impacted the radio transmitter, just missing Kate.

As Santiago got total control of the gun, he kicked Joan away and got off one more wild shot, which caught Joan in the upper thigh. He was about to finish her off when two other shots blasted into his chest.

Reid was kneeling down in the doorway leading down to the lower decks with his rifle still pointed at Santiago, who died on his feet with a look of shocked horror, before falling on the deck.

Halprin came rushing back into the stateroom with his gun drawn, but relaxed once he saw the situation was under control. Kate and Jones were looking after Joan's wound, while Cooper—the techno nerd of the two—was evaluating the damage done to the radio.

"What happened?" Halprin asked.

"I screwed up," Joan said more upset with herself for letting her guard down, then her wounded leg.

"It wasn't your fault," Kate objected to Joan's self imposed blame as the sound of the speedboat returning with Walker echoed out on the water.

Kelly and Fergusen brought Walker into the stateroom, paying no mind to Santiago's dead body, and put him down on a couch near the bar. While Kelly checked out Walker's vital signs, Fergusen went over to tend to Joan's wounds. Walker was badly wounded from the beating he took and barely conscious as he struggled to find his voice.

After a quick assessment of the situation, Halprin took charge and started to bark out orders. "Reid, what is our weapon and ammo status?"

"Still enough to take out an entire army, sir," Reid answered.

"Cooper, what about communications?" Halprin asked next.

"The transmitter is shot, literally," Cooper informed him while noting the irony. "We only have the ability to receive incoming transmissions, sir."

Halprin went over to where Fergusen was tending to Joan's wound using a first aid kit from the yacht. After finishing wrapping a bandage on Joan's leg, he and Kate helped her to sit her by the controls.

"You all right, Major? Hurt badly?" Halprin asked.

"Only my pride."

"Don't even give it a second thought."

Halprin looked over at Santiago's dead body, then over at Reid. "Reid, throw that piece of trash overboard. We are going back to the island."

Walker finally found his voice as he called out to Halprin. "Captain. No. Wait. We got to stop it," he said in a strained, hoarse voice.

Kelly was trying to make Walker as comfortable as possible. Halprin walked over to Walker's side and looked over at Kelly for a prognosis of Walker's condition, and with a slight head shake he indicated that it wasn't good.

"Stop what, Walker," Halprin asked giving him his full attention.

Walker struggled with the words as he sat up to speak. "There is a nuclear sub out there somewhere that's going to launch a warhead at Baghdad when the Nimitz docks at Mahe' tomorrow."

"Shit! They're trying to start World War Three," Halprin exclaimed as he stood up and looked into the faces of everyone, recognizing the severity of the situation.

Everyone all seemed to silently come to the same conclusion that it would be up to them to save the day.

"That is why they wanted the S.M.A.R.T. Station. They must have figured a way to block the detection of a sub launching a warhead, which would make it appear that it came from the Nimitz. By the time anyone figured out what really happened, it would be too late."

"We're going to have to split up," Joan stated as a matter of fact.

Halprin looked at her with the same realization. "I think you might be right."

****

The speedboat floated along side of the yacht. Halprin handed down supplies to Reid and the seven other men who were going to the island in the speedboat. Jones had a two way radio head set from the armory.

Joan, Walker, Cooper, and Kelly remained on the yacht. Cooper had the partner to Jones' radio head set and was inside working on the yacht's radio, while Kelly looked after Walker. Joan was going over the plan with Kate and Halprin.

"I wish there was another way," Kate said, not feeling optimistic that they could save the world.

"If we can't find that sub, then retaking the S.M.A.R.T. Station won't matter." Halprin paused as he looked into Kate's eyes. "I wish you would reconsider and stay on the yacht."

"I might be the only one left with official clearance to contact the White House to explain things. This will be a top priority order and they might not listen to someone not from the station," Kate reasoned.

"You're right. But getting there won't be easy. We may be extremely well armed, but we are also heavily outnumbered," Halprin pointed out.

"Captain Halprin, I'm counting on you to get my station back and set things right."

"We'll make it happen, Major," Halprin said. "Well make it happen."

Kate and Joan looked at each other, seemingly knowing that they might not see each other again.

"I'll see you soon," Kate said first.

"Count on it," Joan assured her.

Kate saluted Joan and she returned it. Halprin took Kate's hand as she stepped down into the speedboat. Halprin saluted Joan before stepping into the speedboat. Reid was at the controls and the boat was running.

"With any luck we should be at the station by dawn. There won't be much time once we're there," Halprin stated.

"We'll find that sub, and do whatever it takes to prevent it from launching any missiles," Joan said.

Halprin gave Reid the signal to get moving. Kate looked back at Joan as the yacht slowly faded from view.

CHAPTER TWENTY-NINE

"Those fools! I cannot believe these incompetents!" Yusov yelled out, enraged as he once again learned of Halprin's escape. "We should launch now."

"We must wait, comrade," Demetri pleaded, trying to calm Yusov down. "We must not be premature or else we will be detected. The Americans have fled the island. They won't present any further complications."

"You are wrong, comrade. You saw this man's profile. They will be back," Yusov said then turned to Nikki and Sonja, who were guarding Neville and Vanderweel. "Take them back with the others."

Nikki and Sonja urged Neville and Vanderweel out of the S.M.A.R.T. Room.

Yusov grabbed a hold of the mysterious gray suitcase from Santiago's yacht and put it down on the computer console and opened it while ranting on. "With only a handful of men, they have twice outwitted my elite squad, killing my strongest man and even managing to retreat on an arms dealer's yacht. But no matter what happens, we will not fail here, today."

Revealed inside the gray suitcase was a one kiloton nuclear bomb with a remote control timer. Yusov's fingers pressed down on the key pad and a digital read out indicated the bomb was armed.

"I'll personally fly this bomb right up Saddam's ass if I have to," Yusov declared as he took out the remote control and put it in his suit jacket pocket.

Hubert walked over to Yusov and saw what was inside the suitcase, shocked by its contents. "Oh God. You're a madman. This whole plot is insane."

Yusov gave Hubert a pissed off look as his eyes squinted together revealing his rage. He had put up with this little man long enough. How could one who was not chosen ever understand that from the ashes of destruction a new world would rise.

Yusov stepped over to Hubert and looked into his eyes as he spoke softly to him. "Say, Governor. Do me a favor and hold onto this bullet for me," Yusov said as he jammed his gun against Hubert's chest and pulled the trigger. The shot rang out in the S.M.A.R.T. Room as Hubert fell dead to the floor. Yusov then turned to Vadmir. "Call Waiting Eagle and tell them to be on the lookout for Santiago's yacht and that it has been taken over by the enemy."

CHAPTER THIRTY

The calm quiet of the early morning hours had once again returned to the marina. It was only two hours before dawn and the only visible signs of life were two island cops posted as sentries on the boardwalk.

On the other end of the boardwalk, down near the boat shed, the dingy speedboat was docked up on the sand where the boardwalk ended--out of sight.

Creeping along the shadow of the boardwalk, Reid and Stark made their way from the boat shed, toward the two sentries. They were both armed with silencer equipped rifles and took positions beneath the raised boardwalk. After sighting in their respective targets, Reid gave the signal and they fired in unison.

Both sentries fell dead to the boardwalk.

Reid looked back toward the boat shed and whistled out to signal the others that the coast was clear.

The boat shed slid open as Reid and Stark hurried back over. They entered the boat shed and Reid reported to Halprin.

"All clear Captain."

"Very good, Sgt. Reid."

Kate was standing by Halprin's side as the rest of the men piled into Joan's jeep, with the exception of Fuller and Miller. Jones had on his radio headset.

The two demolition specialists were just finishing up some unseen project in Halprin's rent-a-car.

Sgt. Fuller, Sgt. Miller are we ready?" Halprin asked, inquiring about their progress.

"Yes, sir. Locked down and ready to roll!" Fuller answered.

"Let's do it then.   No quarter, gentlemen. Full bore. Balls to the wall, all the way." Halprin said then looked at Kate and smiled.

Reid joined Fuller and Miller at Halprin's rent-a-car after trading his weapon for an M-16 with a grenade launcher attached. Fuller got behind the wheel as Reid got in the passenger seat. The windshield had been broken out of the car. Miller joined the others in the jeep after wishing Fuller and Reid good luck with a salute.

The rent-a-car pulled out of the boat shed, followed by Joan's jeep. The two vehicles moved down the road and headed up the hill leading to the S.M.A.R.T. Station.

****

It was just before dawn and Santiago's yacht moved slowly on the water with search lights on as the brightening sky of a new day began.

In the stateroom, Kelly was still looking after Walker, who was conscious but groggy.

"We are almost to the last location the Treasure Seeker reported before losing contact," Joan told Cooper while steering the yacht. "I'm sure that damn sub is hidden around here, somewhere."

"Where do we start looking?" Cooper asked

As Joan grazed out of the windshield, she pointed out in front of her. "There."

She pointed out at a large uninhabited island in front of the yacht.

"The Treasure Seeker's original destination was that island. For hundreds of years it has been a suspected pirate treasure site. The island is made up of underwater caves. The perfect place for a sub to lay low," Joan said as she looked over at Cooper and Kelly. "Ready to get wet?"

****

On the main road to the tracking station, Halprin's rent-a-car was in the lead with Joan's jeep following as the two vehicles moved quickly up the road. The jeep started to fade back as the rent-a-car developed a substantial lead.

Fuller was driving the rent-a-car and there was an impact bomb on the seat between him and Reid, who had his grenade launcher equipped M-16 pointed out the missing windshield.

Up ahead, a formidable roadblock suddenly appeared around a bend in the road. There were two police cars parked nose to nose with two Humvees parked the same behind them, with mercenaries and cops lined up in between the two vehicles. Moulin was in the middle and Garcia and

Sergi were at his side. They were all heavily armed.

Moulin shouted the order to fire as he saw the fast approaching car.

Fuller continued to drive fast, right into the storm of bullets, as Reid returned fire.

"Get ready to jump," Fuller said.

"I going to try and take out those police cars first," Reid said as he pumped two grenades out of the launcher as they closed in on the roadblock.

One of the police cars took a direct hit in the gas tank and exploded in a fireball as the car lifted off the ground and flipped over on its side. Several mercenaries, cops and Sergi were killed in the blast.

Moulin was thrown back in between the two Humvees, which withstood the blast quite well.

As they approached within twenty-five yards of the roadblock, Fuller was struck with two bullets.

Reid tried to grab the wheel from Fuller. "Jump! I'll hold the wheel."

"No. It's too late. Get out!" Fuller didn't wait for Reid to argue with him as he reached over, opened the door and kicked him out of the car.

Fuller floored the vehicle as he yelled loudly.

The rent-a-car rammed into the roadblock with Fuller in it. The explosion was extreme and devastating. The remaining police car was blown to bits along with Garcia and the rest of the mercenaries and cops. The two Humvees were flung into the air and landed on the sides of the road in flaming wrecks.

Reid rolled to his feet as the jeep reached him. He jumped onto the sideboard and held onto the window frame. He was on the passenger side, next to Kate, with Halprin driving.

As they passed through where the roadblock used to be, Moulin was limping up the road, looking behind at the approaching vehicle in a panic. He saw the jeep passing by the flaming Humvees and tried to hurry his pace.

Halprin recognized Moulin and just floored it.

"Die pig!" Halprin said as he ran over the screaming Moulin.

CHAPTER THIRTY-ONE

A large splash of water rose out of the ocean as Cooper and Kelly, outfitted in scuba gear found on the yacht, tumbled over the side and hit the water. They were also equipped with an underwater video camera and a search light, courtesy of Santiago.

Joan was leaning on the railing to help support herself, due to her injury. She hobbled back into the stateroom with the cave island ominously standing out behind the yacht. It was a lifeless rock, one of the many granite islands that made up the Seychelles. Unknown to her, the exception today was a five man squad of mercenaries making their way down toward her position.

They were all armed and wearing scuba gear.

In the stateroom, Walker was over by the communication controls and also had to prop himself up in order to remain on his feet. He had a painful grimace on his face as he leaned on the console while trying to bring up the video feedback from the underwater camera.

"Sgt. Hunt! You shouldn't be on your feet," Joan said as she hobbled in. "You might be bleeding internally."

Walker understood this, but didn't care. "No sweat, Major. I'm fine. Just getting the video now."

There were two Russian assault rifles leaning against the console next to Walker. Joan limped over to Walker and leaned on the console next to him. There was a small monitor screen built into the communication console, displaying the video playback.

****

Kelly and Cooper swam toward the large cavernous underwater caves. Kelly was holding the video camera and Cooper worked the search light as they closed in on what looked big and dark enough to be the entrance to hell.

****

Attracted by the explosion down the road, Yusov and Demetri ran out of the tracking station to the front gate where the other Humvees were parked. The mercenaries standing guard all looked down the road at a large cloud of smoke, coming from where the roadblock was, about two miles away.

"They won't be back, huh," Yusov said sarcastically. "We are launching now."

Yusov headed back in as Demetri stood there for a moment, gazing out at the black cloud.

"They'll be coming. Don't let them through at any cost," Demetri told the mercenaries before heading back inside. He entered the station and detoured down to the cafeteria.

Demetri stood in the cafeteria doorway, surveying the room, which very well contained. Franco, Darius, Nikki and Sonja, and the other mercenaries wearing suits were standing guard over Vanderweel, Neville, and the remaining tracking station and embassy personnel.

"Franco, Sonja. Go outside and take command of the front entrance. We got company coming," Demetri told them.

Vanderweel and Neville looked at each other. They had a good idea who that company was.

Franco and Sonja headed outside as Demetri walked back to the S.M.A.R.T. Room.

Yusov was over by Vadmir asking about the virus when Demetri returned.

"Comrade Vadmir, how much longer until we are ready to launch?" Yusov inquired hastily.

"The virus is ready but the Nimitz is still an hour away from the optimum launch position," Vadmir answered.

"Good enough.   Order the launch," Yusov commanded.

Vadmir did as he was told and called the sub.   "Come in Waiting Eagle.   This is Land Rover.   We are go.   Move into position and fire at will."

****

Deep in the ocean depths, Admiral Jarvet, the Iranian commander of the stolen Typhoon Class Ballistic Missile Submarine, gave the order.   "Move into launch position."

****

The sub's giant propeller started to turn as Cooper and Kelly were exploring the inside of the large cave that hid the sub. Surprised by the subs appearance. The prop wash created an undertow that was beginning to draw them into its blades. As the sub started to emerge from the cave, Cooper and Kelly luckily found refuge in a smaller cave and waited for the submarine to pass.

****

Joan and Walker were brief witnesses to the sight of the sub in the video playback before it was cut off. Joan banged her fist on the monitor screen as Walker saw the reflection of the mercenaries in scuba gear in the windshield. Three of them entered the stateroom, while the other two were still out on the stern. They were armed with automatic weapons.

Walker pushed Joan to the deck as he went for the rifle leaning against the console. He was able to save Joan from the barrage of bullets the three mercenaries unleashed at them, but not himself as he took the brunt of the action, with the bullets penetrating all around the control console. He fell to the deck grabbing his rifle.

Joan reacted quickly as she rolled out along the deck, drawing her pistol and shooting at the mercenaries, taking out two of the three. The third fled back out to the stern.

Unaware of the other two mercenaries already out on the stern, Joan got up and went after the third one. Reaching the stateroom doorway, she shot him as he was turning around to return fire. He then fell dead, backwards and overboard, but the other two mercenaries targeted in on Joan and got the drop on her. She fell back into the stateroom as she took two bullets in the shoulder and one in the stomach. Her pistol fell from her hand and was out of her reach as she lay bleeding to death on the deck.

The two remaining mercenaries entered the stateroom and stood over Joan.

"One tough bitch," one mercenary quipped.

They were about to finish her off when a hail of bullets ripped into both of them, making their bodies dance in bloody death.

Joan rolled onto her stomach and looked back towards the controls and saw Walker, also on his stomach, smoking rifle in hand. Both were both badly wounded and in great pain, functioning only on adrenaline and patriotism.

"We have to call in the coordinates," Joan managed to groan out as she crawled, then managed to get to her feet.

Walker pulled himself up by using the console. He got to his feet and exclaimed in distress at what he saw. "Shit! They got the goddam radio again."

Joan made it over to Walker and was more concerned with what she saw through the windshield, looking out over at the mouth of the cave island. "Never mind the radio, we got to do something about that."

Walker looked out at the clear blue, shallow water that could be seen over the bow. The dark shadow of the sub moved under the water as it emerged from the cave.

"It's moving into launch position. We are too late!" Walker yelled fearfully.

"Maybe not. We can still get in its way," Joan said.

They both realized what they must do as Walker started the engine and Joan took the controls.

****

Out on the water in front of the yacht, the shadow of the sub moved across the water with the yacht in hot pursuit. The yacht moved over the end of the sub and looked like it would easily overtake it.

In the water, near the base of the island, Cooper and Kelly popped up to the surface and bobbed there while watching the yacht move away from them.

****

Joan and Walker clung to the controls as they passed over the back of the sub. They were both close to passing out from shock and barely hanging on, holding onto each other for support, united in their valiant effort to prevent the unthinkable.

"Do you think they've detected us yet?" Walker asked in a painfully strained voice.

"I don't think so. We might be too close," Joan answered with a painful grimace.

****

As the sub moved into open water, with the yacht crossing the half way point of covering it, the top missile hatch started to open as the sub prepared to launch.

Admiral Jarvet stood at the COM as he gave the order to launch still unaware of the presence of the yacht overhead. "Fire missile one."

****

With the yacht now covering three quarters of the sub and the open missile hatch, Joan and Walker clamped their hands together as they made the ultimate sacrifice. The sound of the missile being launched vibrated under the yacht for a moment, before being overwhelmed with the thunderous crash as it broke the bottom of the boat. The top of the missile burst through the stateroom deck as the yacht exploded, blowing up the missile, but preventing the warhead from arming due to the early detonation of the rocket.

The yacht broke in two as it exploded in the middle, with the broken halves sinking down on top of the sub. The debris caused the sub to be wedged in between the rocky island base and another underwater rock formation, immobilizing it.

On top of the water, Cooper and Kelly stood on the rocks of the island shore line, looking out at the giant black cloud of smoke that rose in the air knowing full well what it meant.

****

About five miles away from where the yacht was, the U.S.S. Nimitz was heading for Mahe' and had a view of the smoke cloud on the horizon.

Admiral Nathan Gibson was drinking a cup of coffee as he roamed the bridge. He appeared quite at ease, due to their destination and the news of cooperation with Iraq, but that ease was soon broken.

"Admiral, sir.   We're picking up an explosion on radar and the lookout is reporting smoke off the bow, five miles south west of our position," a radar crewman reported.

The admiral handed his coffee to a crewman. "Pinpoint the location and alert the fighters and the rescue choppers."

CHAPTER THIRTY-TWO

Yusov was anxiously pacing the S.M.A.R.T. Room, awaiting for confirmation of the launch. Demetri stood behind Vadmir, who was confused by his findings.

"I am unable to confirm launch or re-establish communications with Waiting Eagle," Vadmir reported.

Yusov stopped his pacing and stood behind Demetri and Vadmir with a stone cold, hard facial expression. A man on the brink of maniacal collapse.

"Keep trying," Demetri ordered. "They must be out there."

Yusov no longer had any interest in the sub. He knew the he could no longer count on them to complete their objective. It would be left to him. What better way to go then taking as many as one's enemies as possible. It was his time now. Time for rebirth.

****

Franco and Sonja were standing out by the front gate with a dozen heavily armed mercenaries also posted at the gate. Suddenly, the sound of a fast moving vehicle, coming up the road leading to the station, alerted the mercenaries. They all readied themselves, aiming their weapons toward the sound.

Down the road, in front of the mercenaries, Joan's jeep was moving up at breakneck speed, straight for the entrance gate. The mercenaries opened fire on the jeep, but it didn't slow down as it headed right for the Humvees blocking the gate.

The mercenaries all ran for cover as the jeep crashed into the front of the Humvees and flew up over them. The jeep flipped over as it took to the air and landed on its roof in a mangled, screeching wreck.

While the mercenaries were all gathering their wits, Halprin and his men wasted no time as they ran up the road, behind the jeep, shooting at the discombobulated mercenaries. Halprin and Reid were at the point as they led the way in two man teams. Kate and Jones brought up the rear as they all blasted through the gate.

Halprin jumped up on the hood of one of the Humvees and took out three mercenaries with precision accuracy. He then targeted Franco as Franco targeted him, but Halprin was quicker and shot him dead.

Reid and the others took out the rest of the mercenaries with relative ease.

Sonja popped up from behind the other Humvee, opposite Halprin, and was about to shoot him. But Kate was there and shot her several times from across the other Humvee, emptying her gun into Sonja.

Halprin looked over at Kate as he stepped down off the Humvee, then over at Sonja's dead body, realizing Kate had just saved his life.

"I owe you one," Halprin said smiling as he looked back at Kate.

"I'll collect later. What do you say we go put things right!" Kate said cockily.

"Yeah! Time to clean house."

****

Demetri was standing in the S.M.A.R.T. Room doorway, attracted by the confrontation going on outside.

Yusov stood in front of the open suitcase bomb. He closed the case and looked over at Demetri, who was still looking down the hall. He was about to say something when Vadmir, who was unaware of what was going on around him, spoke first.

"Comrade Yusov, Waiting Eagle is back on line. They report some damage, but they still believe they can achieve their objective," Vadmir reported enthusiastically.

Yusov didn't verbally respond, but instead took his gray suitcase in hand. He stood at attention for a moment as he spoke. "From chaos springs rebirth and from Eden's fall the Heavens will rise."

Demetri looked back at Yusov, momentarily forgetting about the sounds of the invasion. "Andrei, don't. There's still time."

****

Halprin and his men entered the station and blasted away two mercenaries by the hallway leading to the cafeteria, forcing a third to flee back there.

"Reid, take half the men and secure that area," Halprin ordered.

"Yes, sir," Reid replied as he led Stark and Fergusen down to the cafeteria as Halprin, Kate, Jones, Miller, and Roth headed for the S.M.A.R.T. Room.

****

Darius and Nikki were holding the tracking station hostages in the cafeteria with only three other mercenaries. Then, the one from the hallway ran in, but was shot from behind and fell dead into the room. There were two cafeteria entrances and Darius and the other mercenaries didn't know whether to concentrate on their attackers or their hostages. They didn't have to think about it for long.

Reid jumped through one entrance as Stark and Fergusen took the other. Reid shot Darius and one of the other mercenaries while Stark and Fergusen took out the other two.

Nikki grabbed hold of Neville and held him in front of her like a human shield.

"Step back or I'll blow his head off!" Nikki threatened.

Reid had Nikki sighted in right between the eyes with his gun. "And you'll be dead one second later. Now give it up. You've nowhere to go. It's over."

Nikki understood this. She let go of Neville, stepped back, then shot herself in the head.

****

Yusov ran down to the offices at the back of the S.M.A.R.T. Room leaving Demetri standing in the middle of the room with his back to the door, staring after his fleeing comrade. Vadmir was still at the computer console and in contact with the submarine.

Kate, Halprin, and his men charged into the room and had the tactical advantage.   Vadmir raised his hands in surrender.

"Live or die, asshole. It's up to you," Halprin said pointing his gun at Demetri, who still hadn't raised his hands.

Demetri went for his gun as he whirled around, but never got it out of his holster. Halprin shot him once between the eyes, then pointed his gun at Vadmir's head.

"Where did that white haired bastard go?" Halprin asked cocking his gun in an effort to show Vadmir that killing him was no big thing.

"Don't kill me," Vadmir pleaded, wanting to live.

"Where did he go?" Halprin insisted.

"That way," Vadmir pointed down toward the end of the room. "He has a nuclear bomb in a gray suitcase."

Halprin turned to Kate. "Call the White House and the Seventh Fleet and let them know what's going on. I'm going after him."

"Watch yourself, Jack," Kate cautioned as Halprin took off after Yusov.

Kate held her gun to Vadmir's head as Jones walked over to the command console. "I want all systems back on line right now or I'm going to blow your head off," Kate jabbed the gun barrel against Vadmir's temple.

"Okay, okay. Don't shoot. I will obey. Everyone wants to blow my head off today."

Jones tried to raise the yacht on the radio head set. "Cooper, come in. Over. Anyone, come in. Over."

Vadmir looked up at Jones and said. "You will not be able to contact your comrades at sea."

"Give me the coordinates of the sub, you son-of-a-bitch," Kate demanded, jabbing her gun barrel against Vadmir's head again.

****

Still stuck between the rocks and the yacht wreckage, the sub slowly began to break free.

CHAPTER THIRTY-THREE

Vice President Kimball was in the White House gym, shooting baskets by himself. He was standing on the free throw line, wearing sweatpants and sweatshirt from his Harvard alma mater, making basket after basket—with no effort. An aide stood under the net, returning the ball to him.

"That is ten in a row, sir. You could have been in the NBA," the aide said, being a good sycophant.

"I used to think if politics didn't work out, I would always have something to fall back on. Now, I just come here to relax when I get something stuck in my head."

"Do you mean the situation with Iraq, sir?"

"I'm happy about the resolution, but concerned with how it came about. I keep thinking back to my Shakespeare and that line from Hamlet." Kimball paused to shoot another basket with a swish. "Something is rotten in the state..."

A phone on the wall behind the aid rang out, cutting off Kimball. A red button was flashing on the phone along with the ringing. The aide picked it up on the third ring and held it out for Kimball.

Kimball let the basketball drop from his hands as he walked over to the phone. "Kimball here," he paused to listen. "Oh my God. Connect her right through to this line, then get me the Admiral of the Nimitz."

****

Kate was in the S.M.A.R.T. Room with Kimball explaining the situation. "That's right, sir. This is a priority one alert. We have a hostile in the water with intentions of launching on Baghdad."

Jones was now sitting where Vadmir was and Stark kept him covered.

****

Admiral Gibson was on the Nimitz bridge awaiting confirmation on the location of the explosion when the Vice President called.

"I want two F-18s armed and on the deck along with a search and rescue chopper," Gibson ordered.

Sir, I have an action alert message coming directly from Vice President Kimball," a communication crewman reported.

Gibson arched an eyebrow. "Put it on the box."

"Aye, sir."

Kimball's voice echoed out over the bridge and everyone paid close attention to what was being said. "Admiral Gibson, this is Vice President Kimball. We have a state of emergency."

"We are somewhat aware of the situation, but don't yet know the particulars. I was just about to send out a reconnaissance mission."

"Very good, Admiral Gibson, but it will no longer be a reconnaissance mission. I'm sending you the coordinates to sink a nuclear sub that's preparing to launch at Baghdad." Kimball's voice echoed out as everyone on the bridge realized the seriousness of the situation.

****

Two F-18 fighter jets, armed with guided missiles took off from the U.S.S. Nimitz.

****

Back on the cave island, Cooper and Kelly climbed to the peak of the small island to gain a better vantage point. They could see the outline of the sub under the water as it slowly worked its way free and started to move into more open water.

CHAPTER THIRTY-FOUR

As Kate was calling the White House, Halprin exited the station through a side embassy exit just as Yusov was pulling away in his Land Rover. Halprin got off a couple of shots, but decided he would be better off giving chase in the Governor's BMW.

The two vehicles raced down the road, leading to the Mahe' International Airport, both moving at dangerously fast speeds. The BMW closed in on the Land Rover and began to ram it from behind, which didn't have much effect on the heavier vehicle. Realizing this, Halprin extended his arm out his window and shot out the two driver's side tires of the Land Rover, causing it to lose control and flip over onto its side.

The BMW came to a skidding stop, almost slamming into the flipped over vehicle. Halprin got out pointing his gun at the Land Rover on its side with the undercarriage facing him. He moved around to the front of the smashed up vehicle as Yusov crawled through the broken-out windshield with the gray suitcase in his hand, along with the remote control in the other.

Yusov held out the remote for Halprin to clearly see that his finger was literally on the button.

"Captain Halprin, at last we formally meet. You've been a real pain in the ass. I am Colonel Yusov and I suggest you lower your weapon. I have an itchy finger."

"Halprin didn't lower his weapon. This was the man with white hair. "I don't care who you are or what you are fighting for. You're dead!"

Halprin's point of vision kept darting back and forth between the detonator and Yusov's face as he began to recall whom Yusov was. In his mind's eye, Halprin actually could see a younger version of Yusov, thirty years ago, as he remembered when he had sighted him through his rifle scope in Vietnam. But now, the image was no longer blurry. Now the face was clearly identifiable. The circle was complete.

Yusov held his ground and remained focused on his objective. "Captain Halprin, I don't understand why you want to stop me. I'm doing your country a great favor. Your enemies will be eliminated. You will be a hero and I will be reborn."

"You can't possibly believe that."

****

The two F-18 fighters jets passed over the cave island with Cooper and Kelly still standing on the peak, shooting their weapons with no effect at the submerged submarine.

Under the water, the sub's missile hatches opened as it prepared to launch more of its missiles.

The lead fighter pilot called the Nimitz to report on their search. "Mother Hen, this is Baby Bird. We have acquired the target and are preparing to drop our eggs."

Two guided missiles each dropped from the F-18's as they passed by the island. Both hit the water smoothly and quickly slammed into the side of the sub, blowing it up while causing a shock wave that knocked Cooper and Kelly to the ground.

****

The percussion from the sub explosion rang out so loud that it was heard and felt all the way back on Mahe'. This distracted Yusov's attention as he turned his head toward the sound.

Halprin held his ground and seized the opportunity to make his move as he shot Yusov's hand holding the detonator. The detonator fell from Yusov's bloodied hand, still intact, and hit the ground at his feet.

Yusov dropped the gray suitcase as he held onto his wounded hand. He looked at Halprin with a fiery rage in his eyes.

"I know who you are," Halprin said holding his gun on Yusov. "Vietnam! Sixty-eight! Tet Offensive! I was there! You were there too! I have been searching for you in my dreams for so long, but you don't matter anymore. I'm through chasing ghosts from my past. You are just history now."

Yusov's rage piqued as he went for his pistol. He managed to get it out, but that was it.

Halprin unloaded his pistol into Yusov, who refused to go down until the gun was empty. He stood there for a few seconds before falling backwards to the ground. Dead.

Halprin looked up at the clear blue sky as the F-18 fighters flew past the island, returning to the Nimitz. Halprin saluted the jets and stood there knowing that for the moment the world was once again safe from the madmen who would see it destroyed.

CHAPTER THIRTY-FIVE

A long parade of cars and limousines were lined up along the road leading to Arlington National Cemetery. The Presidential Seal stood out on one of the many limousines guarded by motorcycle units. The media was also present in force, covering the high profile event, with over a dozen news vans parked on the lawn in front of the cemetery.

Prime time newscaster John Abrams was there covering the big event while standing on top of a news van along with his camera man. The media was only permitted to cover the memorial service, being held for those who died defending their country, from out on the road.   But the resourceful newshounds always managed to get the shot.

With a view of the cemetery behind him, John Abrams filled the world in on what had happened. "It has been one of the most dramatic events in military history, since the Cuban Missile Crisis. A ruthless band of mercenaries—led by a disgraced ex-Russian Colonel and backed by an ultra radical faction of the Iranian government—has turned out to be responsible for the U.N. Inspection Team ambush in Iraq, three weeks ago.   The mercenaries planned on using the incident to try and start World War Three by launching a nuclear warhead at Baghdad from a hidden Russian submarine, near the Seychelles Islands in the Indian ocean,   off   the   coast   of   Africa.   The mercenaries then took over a U.S. S.M.A.R.T. satellite tracking station, with the help of a corrupt Governor and police force, on the main island, Mahe', in order to prevent the true origin of the launch from being discovered. Thereby, making it appear that the Seventh Fleet did it in retaliation for the U.N. Inspection Team ambush."

A full scale military funeral was taking place behind Abrams while he reported the news. "A memorial service is being held today in remembrance of the brave men and women of the Armed Forces who gave their lives to prevent the launch and stop the unthinkable. President Kimball, whose succession into office came after ex-President Robbins awoke from his coma and stepped down due to his health, is giving the memoriam."

Abrams turned away from his cameraman to look back at the funeral service so that they could zoom in up close for the millions viewing at home.

President Kimball stood in front of a large crowd of mourners, the picture of strength and compassion. He was just finishing the memorial services. "So we honor the memory of those brave souls who gave their lives to preserve world peace. We shall forever hold them in our hearts and memories for their great sacrifice above and beyond the call of duty. Amen."

Halprin and Kate were among the mourners along with the other survivors from Halprin's unit. While Halprin appeared to be holding back his emotions and remained dry eyed, Kate was unable to hold back the tears sliding down her cheeks.

Kimball was making his way through the grieving family members of Joan, Parker and the others as they all received American flags.

Halprin and Kate stood tall as Kimball made his way over to them. They both saluted him and shook his hand.

"Your country owes you and your men a great debt of gratitude, Captain Halprin," Kimball praised.

"We were just doing our job, sir," Halprin said remaining humble. "And we couldn't have done it without the others of our group."

"Yes, of course. I personally thank you all for your courage and devotion. You will all be honored."

An aide urged Kimball through the crowd and Kimball saluted both Halprin and Kate before moving on.

Halprin and Kate remained behind while all the other mourners started to leave. Soon they were the only ones left standing in front of the memorial plaque naming the dead.

"You were the best there was. I'll miss you all," Halprin said to his fallen friends. "But know that none of you died in vain," he finished. Choking back his emotions.

"I'll miss you, Joan. You were a tough bitch," Kate managed to inject, bringing a small smile to her teary eyed cheeks. Halprin was also moved by this, and a single tear also formed and ran down his cheek. They   both   saluted   their fallen friends before turning and walking away with the long rows of white tombstones standing out behind them.